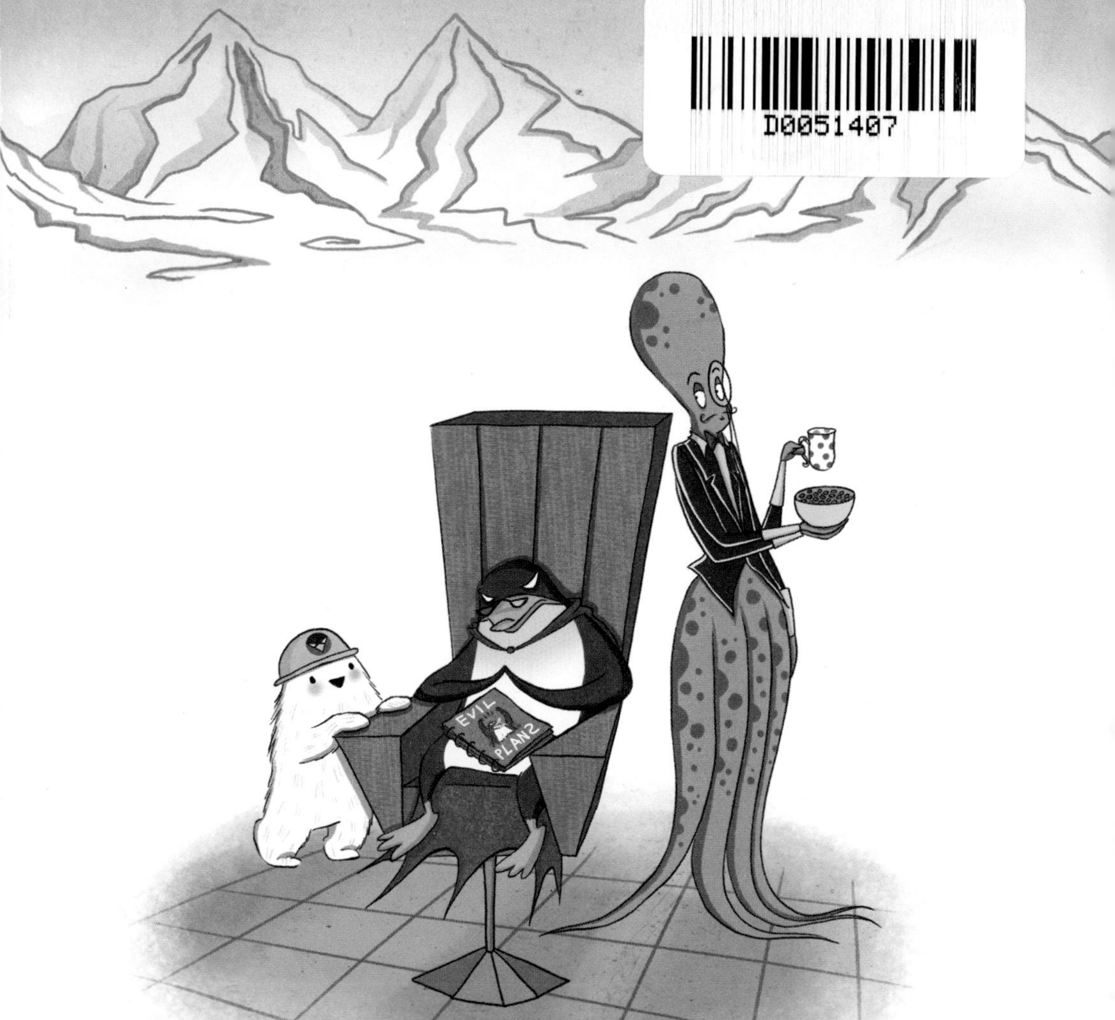
EVIL PLANS

EVIL EMPEROR PENGUIN

LAURA ELLEN ANDERSON

FICKLING
dfb
David Fickling Books
the PHOENIX
SCHOLASTIC

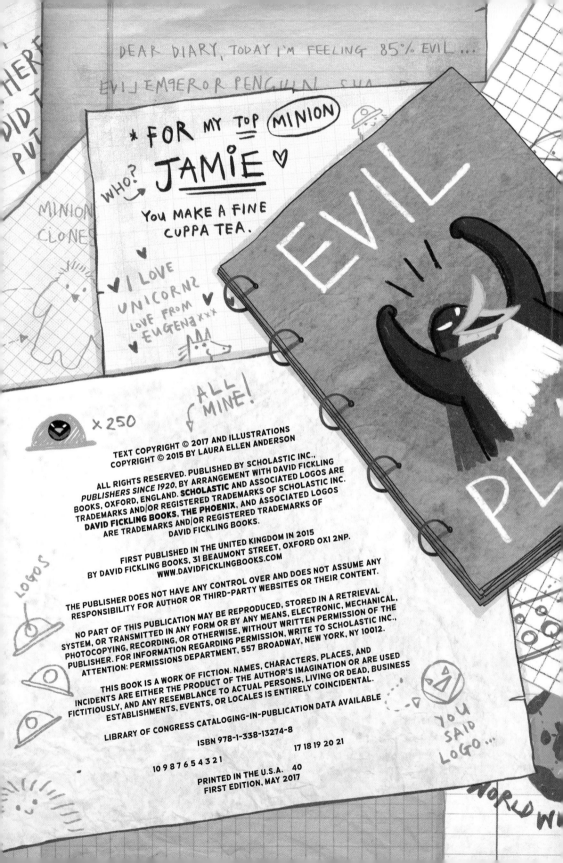

DEAR DIARY, TODAY I'M FEELING 85% EVIL...

EVIL EMPEROR PENGUIN SHA

*FOR MY TOP MINION
WHO? → JAMIE ♡
YOU MAKE A FINE CUPPA TEA.
♥ I LOVE UNICORNS
LOVE FROM EUGENE xxx

MINION CLONES

ALL MINE!
x 250

FIRST PUBLISHED IN THE UNITED KINGDOM IN 2015 BY DAVID FICKLING BOOKS, 31 BEAUMONT STREET, OXFORD OX1 2NP. WWW.DAVIDFICKLINGBOOKS.COM

LIBRARY OF CONGRESS CATALOGING-IN-PUBLICATION DATA AVAILABLE

ISBN 978-1-338-13274-8

10 9 8 7 6 5 4 3 2 1   17 18 19 20 21

PRINTED IN THE U.S.A.   40
FIRST EDITION, MAY 2017

LOGOS

YOU SAID LOGO...

WORLD W

EVIL PL

CONTENTS OF EVIL

EUGENE SAYS HI!

e.e.p.

END

FLYING POD OF EVIL

STUPID CAT

NUMBER 8 RAN OUT OF TEABAGS

SOON THE WORLD I WILL RULE

LASER EYES

BE MINE!!

MWAHAHA HAR HAR!!!

TIME TO CONQUER YOU ALL!!!

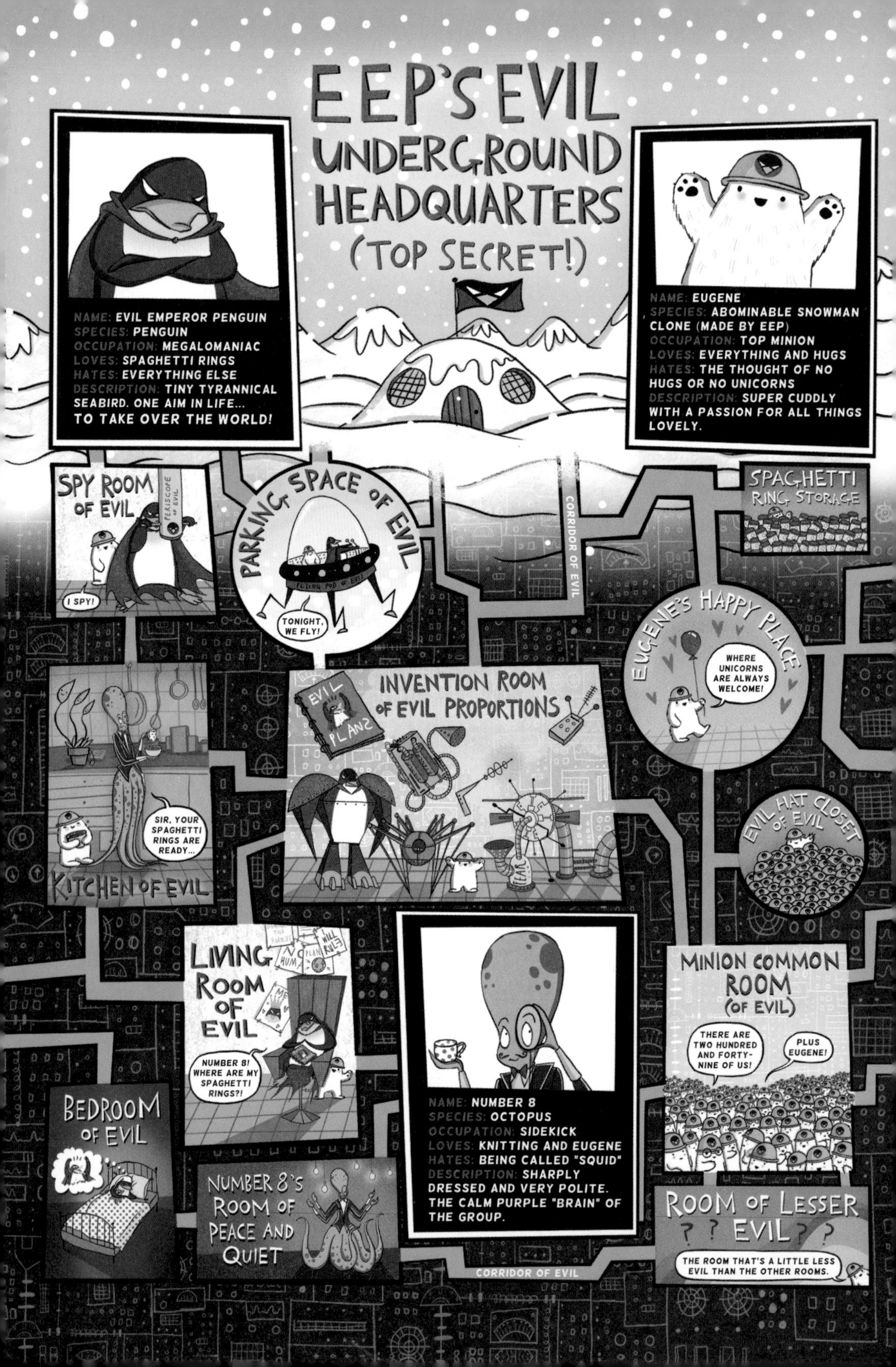
EEP'S EVIL UNDERGROUND HEADQUARTERS
(TOP SECRET!)
NAME: EVIL EMPEROR PENGUIN
SPECIES: PENGUIN
OCCUPATION: MEGALOMANIAC
LOVES: SPAGHETTI RINGS
HATES: EVERYTHING ELSE
DESCRIPTION: TINY TYRANNICAL SEABIRD. ONE AIM IN LIFE... TO TAKE OVER THE WORLD!
NAME: EUGENE
SPECIES: ABOMINABLE SNOWMAN CLONE (MADE BY EEP)
OCCUPATION: TOP MINION
LOVES: EVERYTHING AND HUGS
HATES: THE THOUGHT OF NO HUGS OR NO UNICORNS
DESCRIPTION: SUPER CUDDLY WITH A PASSION FOR ALL THINGS LOVELY.
SPY ROOM OF EVIL
PERISCOPE OF EVIL
I SPY!
PARKING SPACE OF EVIL
FLYING POD OF EVIL
TONIGHT, WE FLY!
CORRIDOR OF EVIL
SPAGHETTI RING STORAGE
EUGENE'S HAPPY PLACE
WHERE UNICORNS ARE ALWAYS WELCOME!
SIR, YOUR SPAGHETTI RINGS ARE READY...
KITCHEN OF EVIL
INVENTION ROOM OF EVIL PROPORTIONS
EVIL PLANS
FEAR
EVIL HAT CLOSET OF EVIL
LIVING ROOM OF EVIL
NUMBER 8! WHERE ARE MY SPAGHETTI RINGS?!
NAME: NUMBER 8
SPECIES: OCTOPUS
OCCUPATION: SIDEKICK
LOVES: KNITTING AND EUGENE
HATES: BEING CALLED "SQUID"
DESCRIPTION: SHARPLY DRESSED AND VERY POLITE. THE CALM PURPLE "BRAIN" OF THE GROUP.
MINION COMMON ROOM (OF EVIL)
THERE ARE TWO HUNDRED AND FORTY-NINE OF US!
PLUS EUGENE!
BEDROOM OF EVIL
NUMBER 8'S ROOM OF PEACE AND QUIET
CORRIDOR OF EVIL
ROOM OF LESSER ? ? EVIL ? ?
THE ROOM THAT'S A LITTLE LESS EVIL THAN THE OTHER ROOMS.

A Stitch in Time

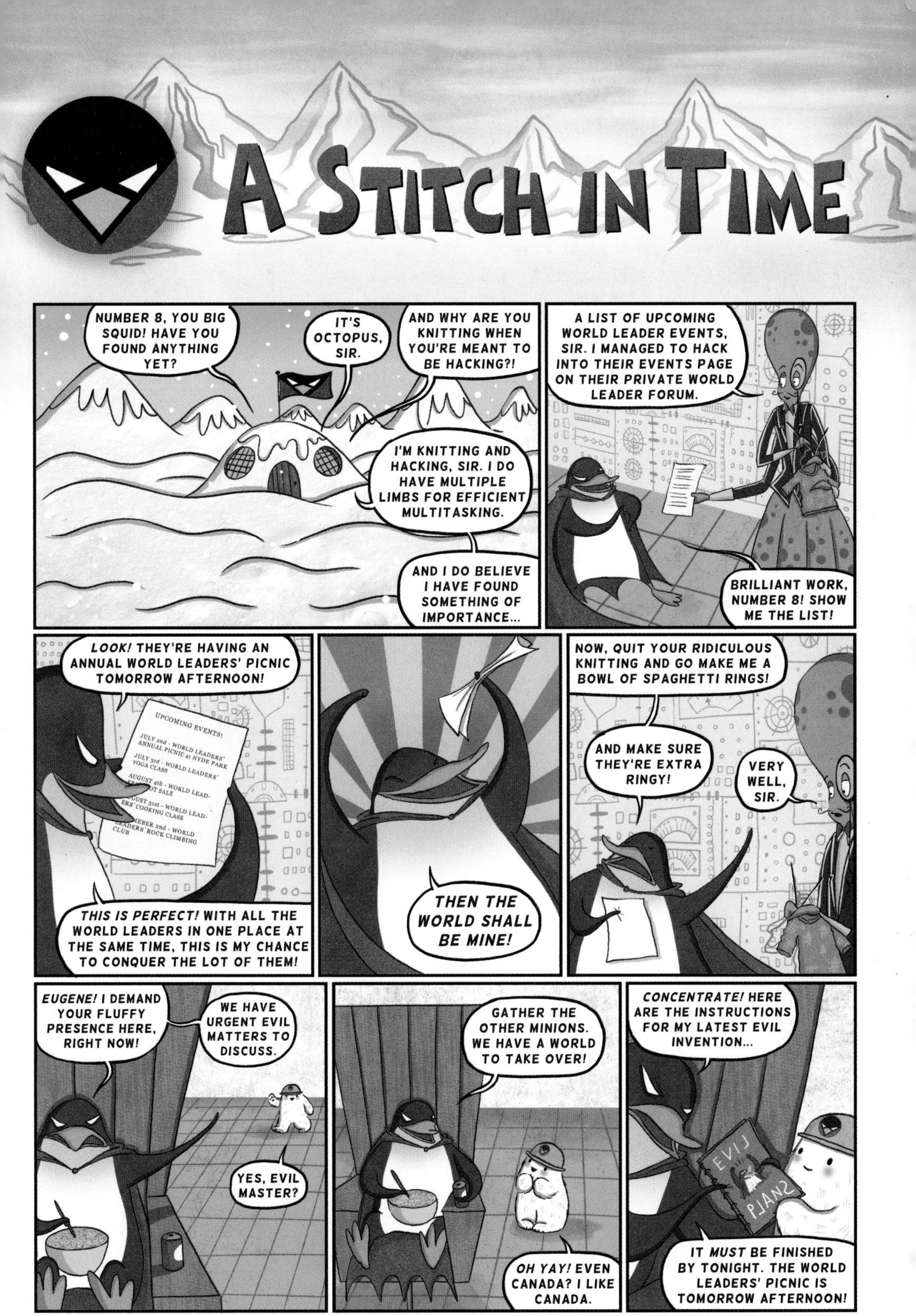

NUMBER 8, YOU BIG SQUID! HAVE YOU FOUND ANYTHING YET?
IT'S OCTOPUS, SIR.
AND WHY ARE YOU KNITTING WHEN YOU'RE MEANT TO BE HACKING?!
I'M KNITTING AND HACKING, SIR. I DO HAVE MULTIPLE LIMBS FOR EFFICIENT MULTITASKING.
AND I DO BELIEVE I HAVE FOUND SOMETHING OF IMPORTANCE...
A LIST OF UPCOMING WORLD LEADER EVENTS, SIR. I MANAGED TO HACK INTO THEIR EVENTS PAGE ON THEIR PRIVATE WORLD LEADER FORUM.
BRILLIANT WORK, NUMBER 8! SHOW ME THE LIST!
LOOK! THEY'RE HAVING AN ANNUAL WORLD LEADERS' PICNIC TOMORROW AFTERNOON!
UPCOMING EVENTS!
JULY 2nd - WORLD LEADERS' ANNUAL PICNIC at HYDE PARK
JULY 3rd - WORLD LEADERS' YOGA CLASS
AUGUST 4th - WORLD LEAD-
ERS' COOKING CLASS
LEADERS' ROCK CLIMBING CLUB
THIS IS PERFECT! WITH ALL THE WORLD LEADERS IN ONE PLACE AT THE SAME TIME, THIS IS MY CHANCE TO CONQUER THE LOT OF THEM!
THEN THE WORLD SHALL BE MINE!
NOW, QUIT YOUR RIDICULOUS KNITTING AND GO MAKE ME A BOWL OF SPAGHETTI RINGS!
AND MAKE SURE THEY'RE EXTRA RINGY!
VERY WELL, SIR.
EUGENE! I DEMAND YOUR FLUFFY PRESENCE HERE, RIGHT NOW!
WE HAVE URGENT EVIL MATTERS TO DISCUSS.
YES, EVIL MASTER?
GATHER THE OTHER MINIONS. WE HAVE A WORLD TO TAKE OVER!
OH YAY! EVEN CANADA? I LIKE CANADA.
CONCENTRATE! HERE ARE THE INSTRUCTIONS FOR MY LATEST EVIL INVENTION...
EVIL PLANS
IT MUST BE FINISHED BY TONIGHT. THE WORLD LEADERS' PICNIC IS TOMORROW AFTERNOON!

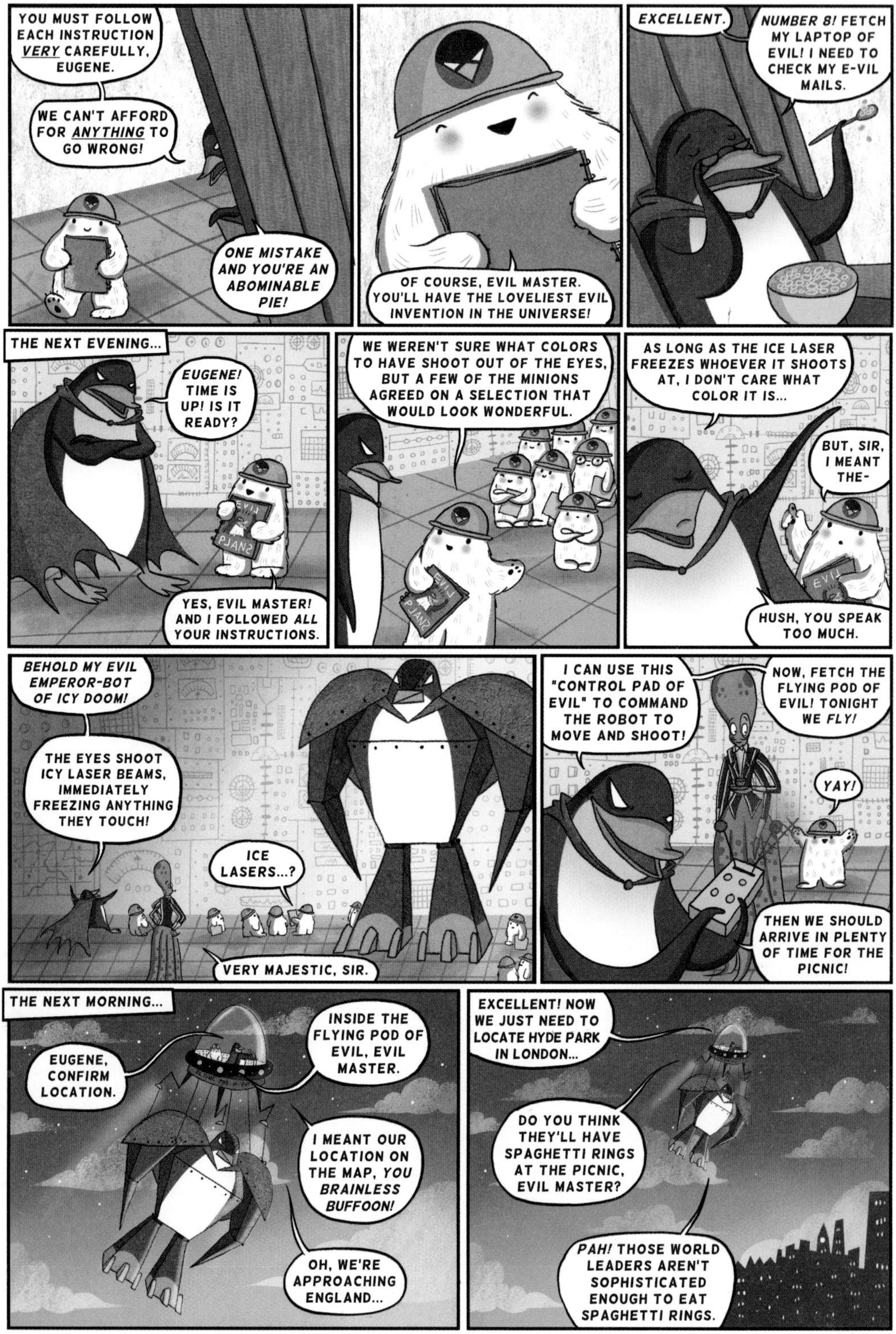

YOU MUST FOLLOW EACH INSTRUCTION VERY CAREFULLY, EUGENE.
WE CAN'T AFFORD FOR ANYTHING TO GO WRONG!
ONE MISTAKE AND YOU'RE AN ABOMINABLE PIE!
OF COURSE, EVIL MASTER. YOU'LL HAVE THE LOVELIEST EVIL INVENTION IN THE UNIVERSE!
EXCELLENT.
NUMBER 8! FETCH MY LAPTOP OF EVIL! I NEED TO CHECK MY E-VIL MAILS.
THE NEXT EVENING...
EUGENE! TIME IS UP! IS IT READY?
EVIL PLANS
YES, EVIL MASTER! AND I FOLLOWED ALL YOUR INSTRUCTIONS.
WE WEREN'T SURE WHAT COLORS TO HAVE SHOOT OUT OF THE EYES, BUT A FEW OF THE MINIONS AGREED ON A SELECTION THAT WOULD LOOK WONDERFUL.
AS LONG AS THE ICE LASER FREEZES WHOEVER IT SHOOTS AT, I DON'T CARE WHAT COLOR IT IS...
BUT, SIR, I MEANT THE-
HUSH, YOU SPEAK TOO MUCH.
BEHOLD MY EVIL EMPEROR-BOT OF ICY DOOM!
THE EYES SHOOT ICY LASER BEAMS, IMMEDIATELY FREEZING ANYTHING THEY TOUCH!
ICE LASERS...?
VERY MAJESTIC, SIR.
I CAN USE THIS "CONTROL PAD OF EVIL" TO COMMAND THE ROBOT TO MOVE AND SHOOT!
NOW, FETCH THE FLYING POD OF EVIL! TONIGHT WE FLY!
YAY!
THEN WE SHOULD ARRIVE IN PLENTY OF TIME FOR THE PICNIC!
THE NEXT MORNING...
EUGENE, CONFIRM LOCATION.
INSIDE THE FLYING POD OF EVIL, EVIL MASTER.
I MEANT OUR LOCATION ON THE MAP, YOU BRAINLESS BUFFOON!
OH, WE'RE APPROACHING ENGLAND...
EXCELLENT! NOW WE JUST NEED TO LOCATE HYDE PARK IN LONDON...
DO YOU THINK THEY'LL HAVE SPAGHETTI RINGS AT THE PICNIC, EVIL MASTER?
PAH! THOSE WORLD LEADERS AREN'T SOPHISTICATED ENOUGH TO EAT SPAGHETTI RINGS.

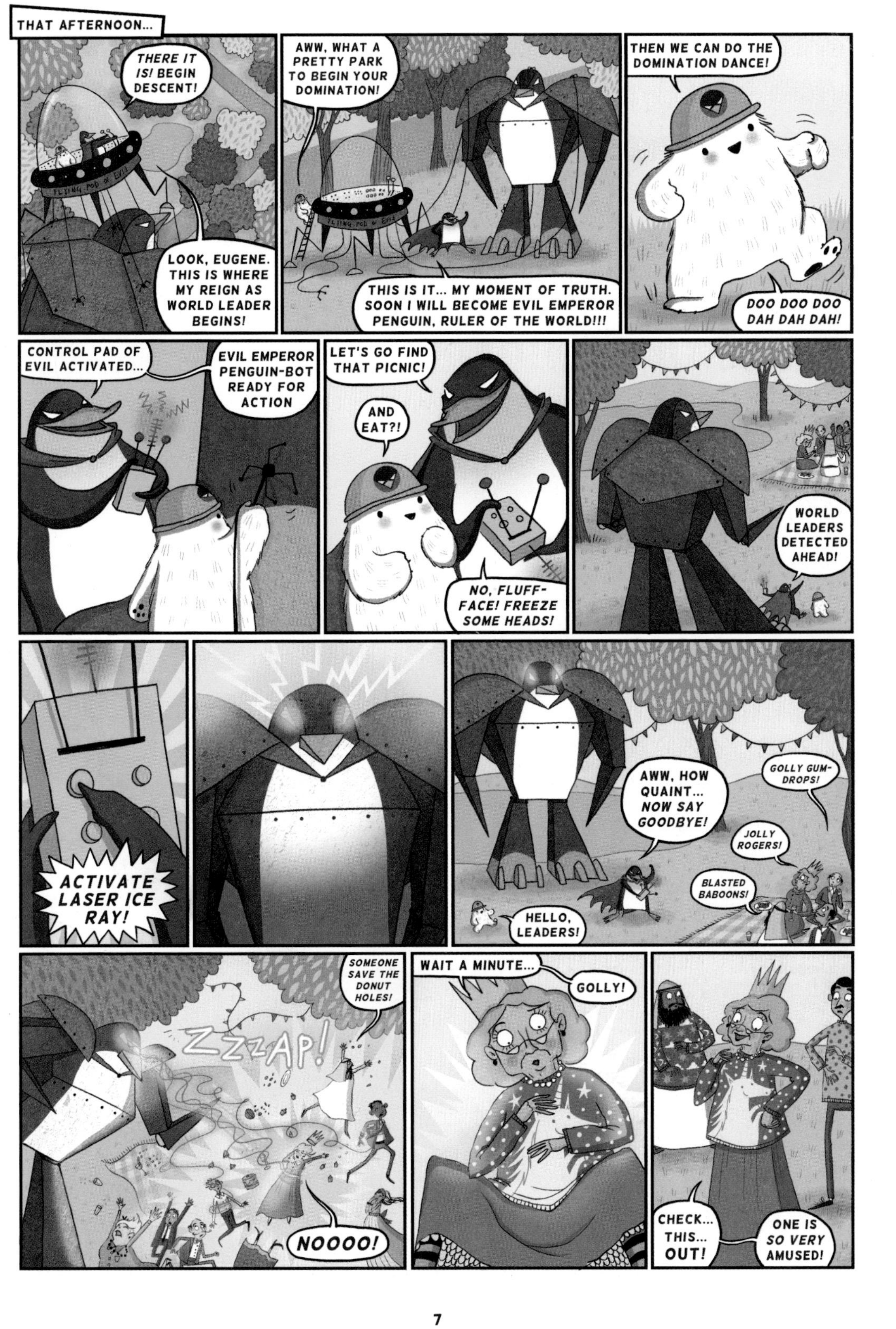
THAT AFTERNOON...
THERE IT IS! BEGIN DESCENT!
LOOK, EUGENE. THIS IS WHERE MY REIGN AS WORLD LEADER BEGINS!
AWW, WHAT A PRETTY PARK TO BEGIN YOUR DOMINATION!
THIS IS IT... MY MOMENT OF TRUTH. SOON I WILL BECOME EVIL EMPEROR PENGUIN, RULER OF THE WORLD!!!
THEN WE CAN DO THE DOMINATION DANCE!
DOO DOO DOO DAH DAH DAH!
CONTROL PAD OF EVIL ACTIVATED...
EVIL EMPEROR PENGUIN-BOT READY FOR ACTION
LET'S GO FIND THAT PICNIC!
AND EAT?!
NO, FLUFF-FACE! FREEZE SOME HEADS!
WORLD LEADERS DETECTED AHEAD!
ACTIVATE LASER ICE RAY!
AWW, HOW QUAINT... NOW SAY GOODBYE!
GOLLY GUM-DROPS!
JOLLY ROGERS!
BLASTED BABOONS!
HELLO, LEADERS!
ZZZAP!
SOMEONE SAVE THE DONUT HOLES!
NOOOO!
WAIT A MINUTE...
GOLLY!
CHECK... THIS... OUT!
ONE IS SO VERY AMUSED!

THAT TERRIFYING PENGUIN ROBOT JUST KNITTED US THE *BEST SWEATERS* I'VE EVER SEEN!

IT'S SO SOFT!

MINE HAS ELBOW PATCHES!

OOO! I WANT ONE! SHOOT ME, O MIGHTY SWEATER-MAKING PENGUIN-BOT!

WHAT THE...

WHAT?!

EUGENE...

PLEASE TELL ME WHY MY EVIL EMPEROR PENGUIN-BOT OF DOOM IS FIRING *KNITTED SWEATERS!*

I FOLLOWED THE INSTRUCTIONS WORD FOR WORD, EVIL MASTER. HONESTLY!

NUMBER 8!!! CAN YOU PLEASE FIND OUT WHY MY MINIONS ARE INCAPABLE OF CREATING *ANYTHING?!*

WHAT'S THE PROBLEM, SIR?

THE PROBLEM, SQUID-FACE, IS THAT MY EVIL WEAPON IS CREATING *SWEATERS* INSTEAD OF MASS DESTRUCTION!

I'LL INVESTIGATE, SIR...

EUGENE, I'VE SPOKEN TO NUMBER 8...

EUGENE?

WHERE'S THE CONTROL PAD OF EV-

OH MY GOSH, IT MAKES COZY HATS TOO!

I *HAVE* TO GET ME ONE OF THOSE!

AREN'T YOU SUCH A WONDERFUL PENGUIN FOR DOING THIS!

SIR, NUMBER 8 HERE...

IT APPEARS MY WEEKLY KNITTING MAGAZINE WAS TUCKED INSIDE YOUR BOOK OF EVIL PLANS.

WHAT?!

EXPLAIN. THEY'RE GETTING AFFECTIONATE HERE...

EUGENE *MAY* HAVE COMBINED YOUR EVIL INSTRUCTIONS WITH THE KNITTED SWEATER INSTRUCTIONS. THIS *COULD* EXPLAIN THE MIX-UP...

EUGENE! WE NEED TO TALK!

I KNOW WHAT'LL CHEER YOU UP, EVIL MASTER!

BEEP!

WAIT, EUGENE! NO!

THE WORLD NEWS

LOVELIEST PENGUIN IN THE WORLD MAKES BEAUTIFULLY KNITTED SWEATERS FOR DELIGHTED WORLD LEADERS.

A lovely penguin approa world leader and s jump at th to th deli

HAVE NO FEAR

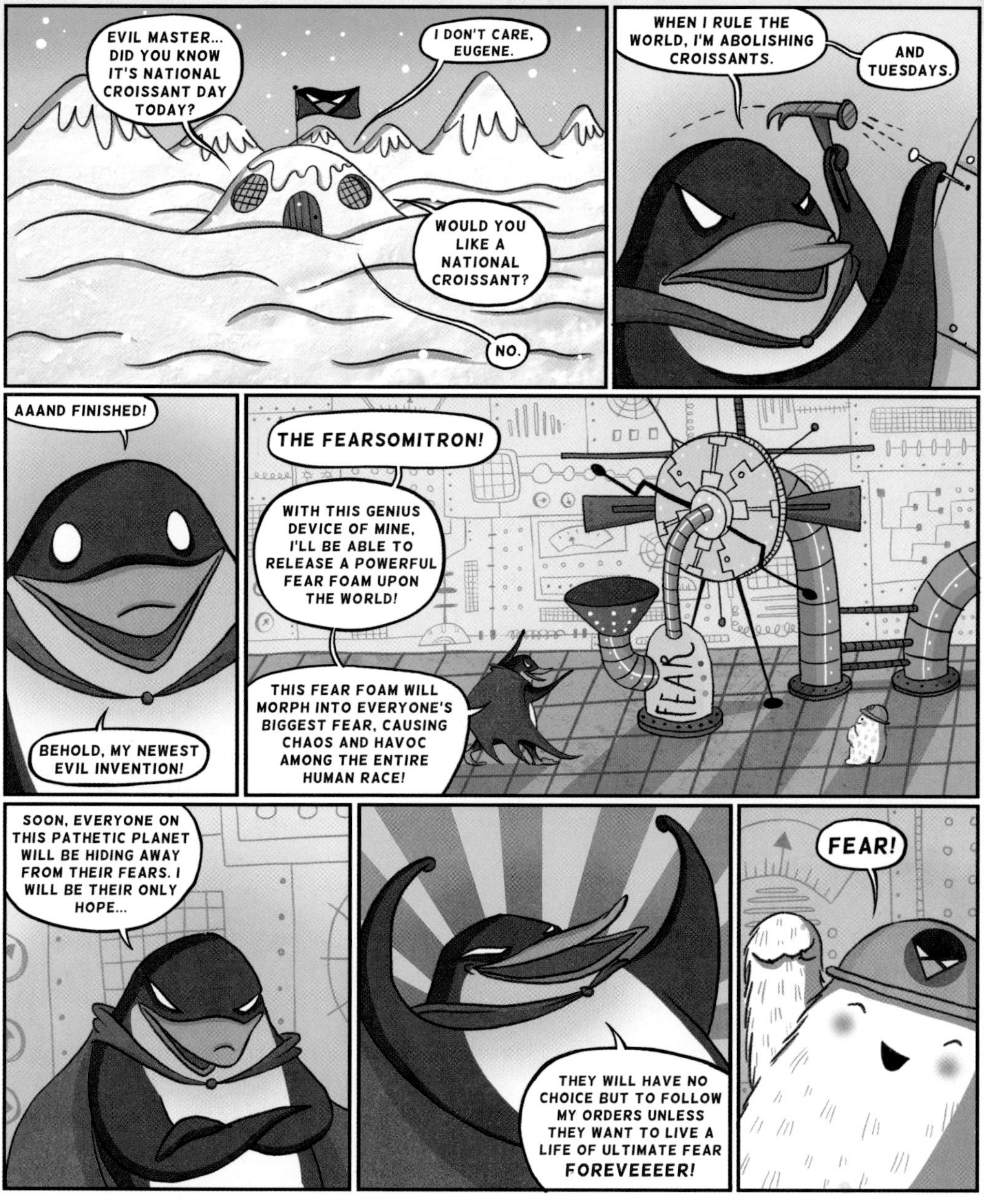
EVIL MASTER... DID YOU KNOW IT'S NATIONAL CROISSANT DAY TODAY?
I DON'T CARE, EUGENE.
WOULD YOU LIKE A NATIONAL CROISSANT?
NO.
WHEN I RULE THE WORLD, I'M ABOLISHING CROISSANTS.
AND TUESDAYS.
AAAND FINISHED!
BEHOLD, MY NEWEST EVIL INVENTION!
THE FEARSOMITRON!
WITH THIS GENIUS DEVICE OF MINE, I'LL BE ABLE TO RELEASE A POWERFUL FEAR FOAM UPON THE WORLD!
THIS FEAR FOAM WILL MORPH INTO EVERYONE'S BIGGEST FEAR, CAUSING CHAOS AND HAVOC AMONG THE ENTIRE HUMAN RACE!
FEAR
SOON, EVERYONE ON THIS PATHETIC PLANET WILL BE HIDING AWAY FROM THEIR FEARS. I WILL BE THEIR ONLY HOPE...
THEY WILL HAVE NO CHOICE BUT TO FOLLOW MY ORDERS UNLESS THEY WANT TO LIVE A LIFE OF ULTIMATE FEAR FOREVEEEER!
FEAR!

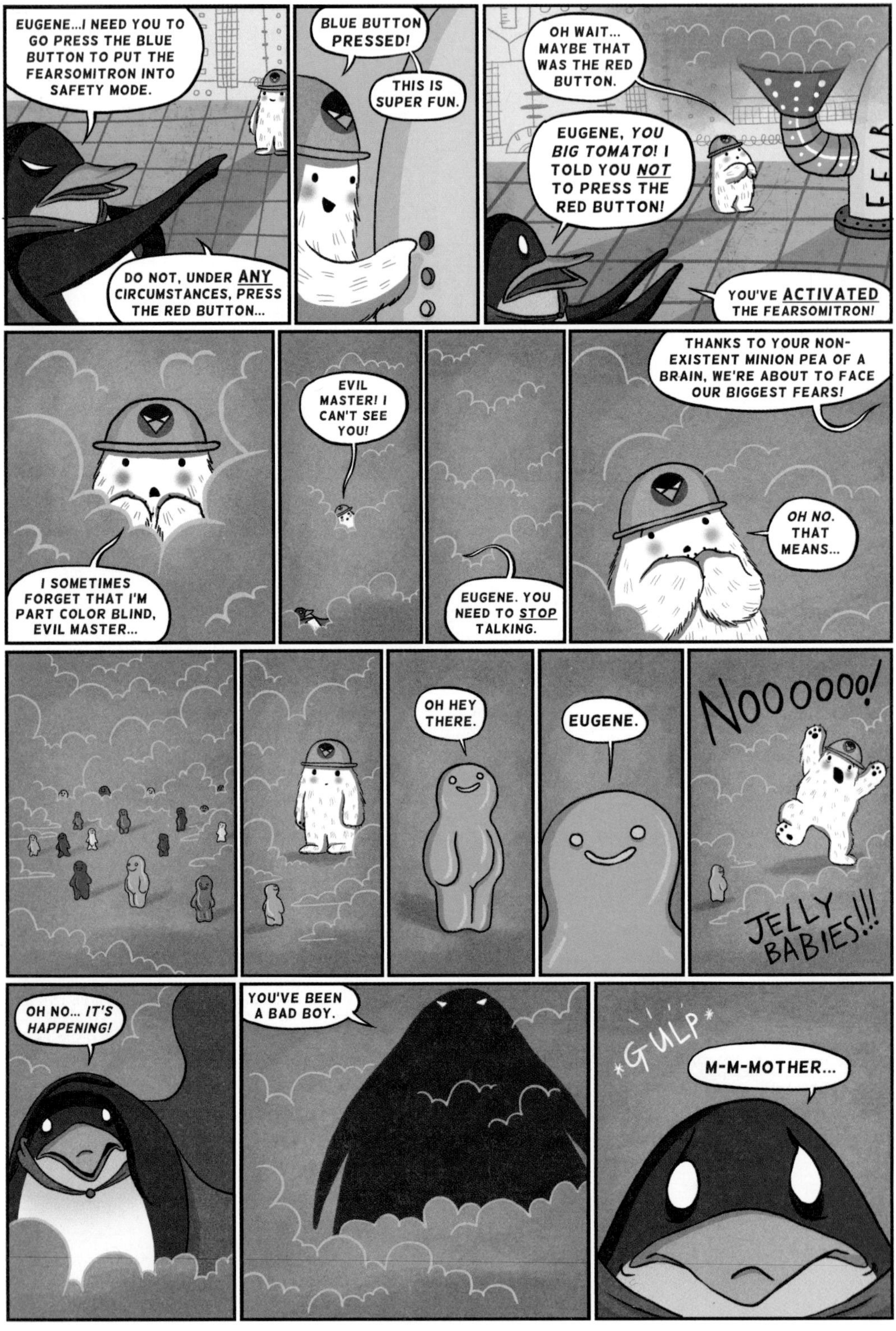
EUGENE...I NEED YOU TO GO PRESS THE BLUE BUTTON TO PUT THE FEARSOMITRON INTO SAFETY MODE.
DO NOT, UNDER ANY CIRCUMSTANCES, PRESS THE RED BUTTON...
BLUE BUTTON PRESSED!
THIS IS SUPER FUN.
OH WAIT... MAYBE THAT WAS THE RED BUTTON.
EUGENE, YOU BIG TOMATO! I TOLD YOU NOT TO PRESS THE RED BUTTON!
FEAR
YOU'VE ACTIVATED THE FEARSOMITRON!
I SOMETIMES FORGET THAT I'M PART COLOR BLIND, EVIL MASTER...
EVIL MASTER! I CAN'T SEE YOU!
EUGENE. YOU NEED TO STOP TALKING.
THANKS TO YOUR NON-EXISTENT MINION PEA OF A BRAIN, WE'RE ABOUT TO FACE OUR BIGGEST FEARS!
OH NO. THAT MEANS...
OH HEY THERE.
EUGENE.
Noooooo!
JELLY BABIES!!!
OH NO... IT'S HAPPENING!
YOU'VE BEEN A BAD BOY.
GULP
M-M-MOTHER...

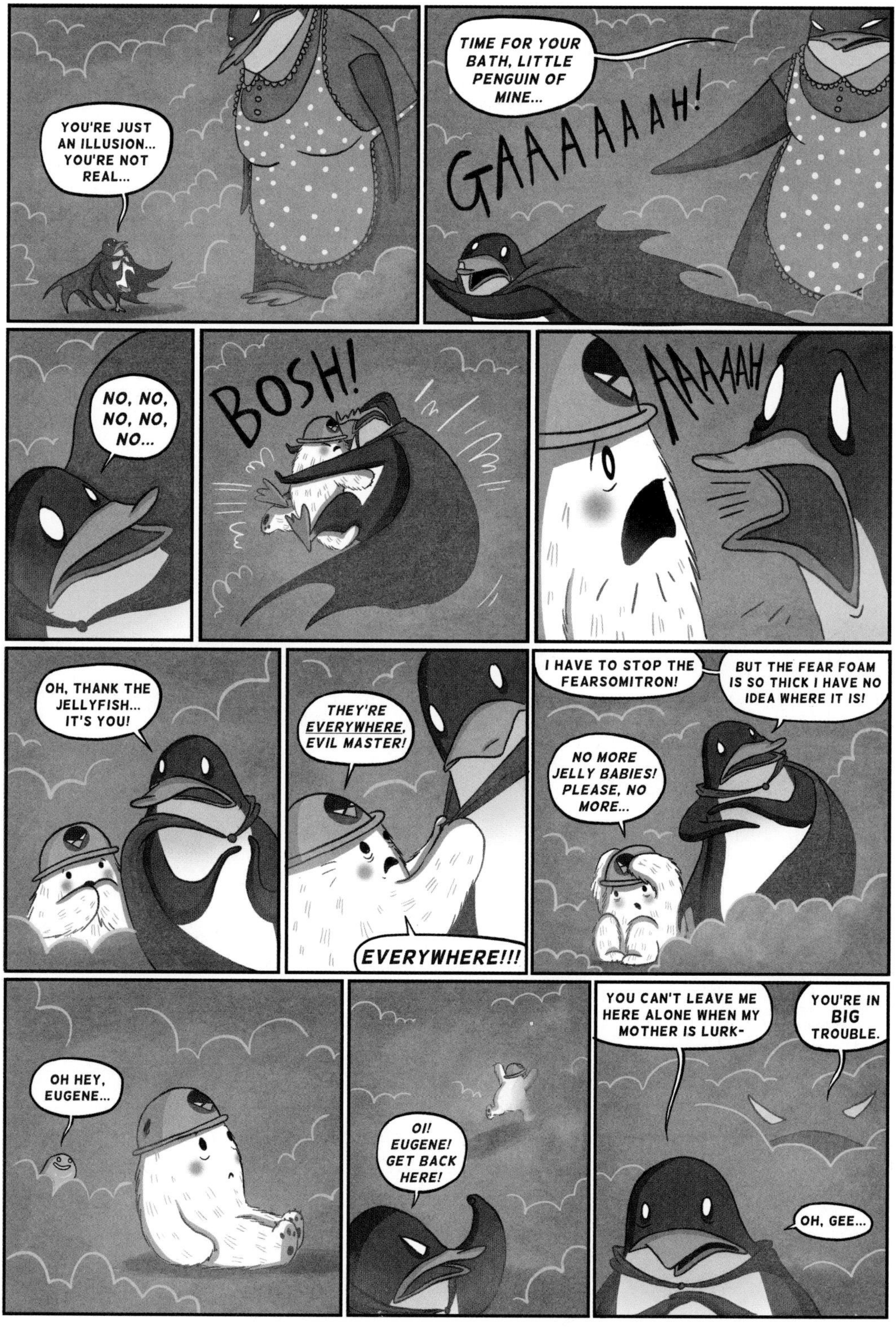
YOU'RE JUST AN ILLUSION... YOU'RE NOT REAL...
TIME FOR YOUR BATH, LITTLE PENGUIN OF MINE...
GAAAAAAH!
NO, NO, NO, NO, NO...
BOSH!
AAAAH
OH, THANK THE JELLYFISH... IT'S YOU!
THEY'RE EVERYWHERE, EVIL MASTER!
EVERYWHERE!!!
I HAVE TO STOP THE FEARSOMITRON!
BUT THE FEAR FOAM IS SO THICK I HAVE NO IDEA WHERE IT IS!
NO MORE JELLY BABIES! PLEASE, NO MORE...
OH HEY, EUGENE...
OI! EUGENE! GET BACK HERE!
YOU CAN'T LEAVE ME HERE ALONE WHEN MY MOTHER IS LURK-
YOU'RE IN BIG TROUBLE.
OH, GEE...

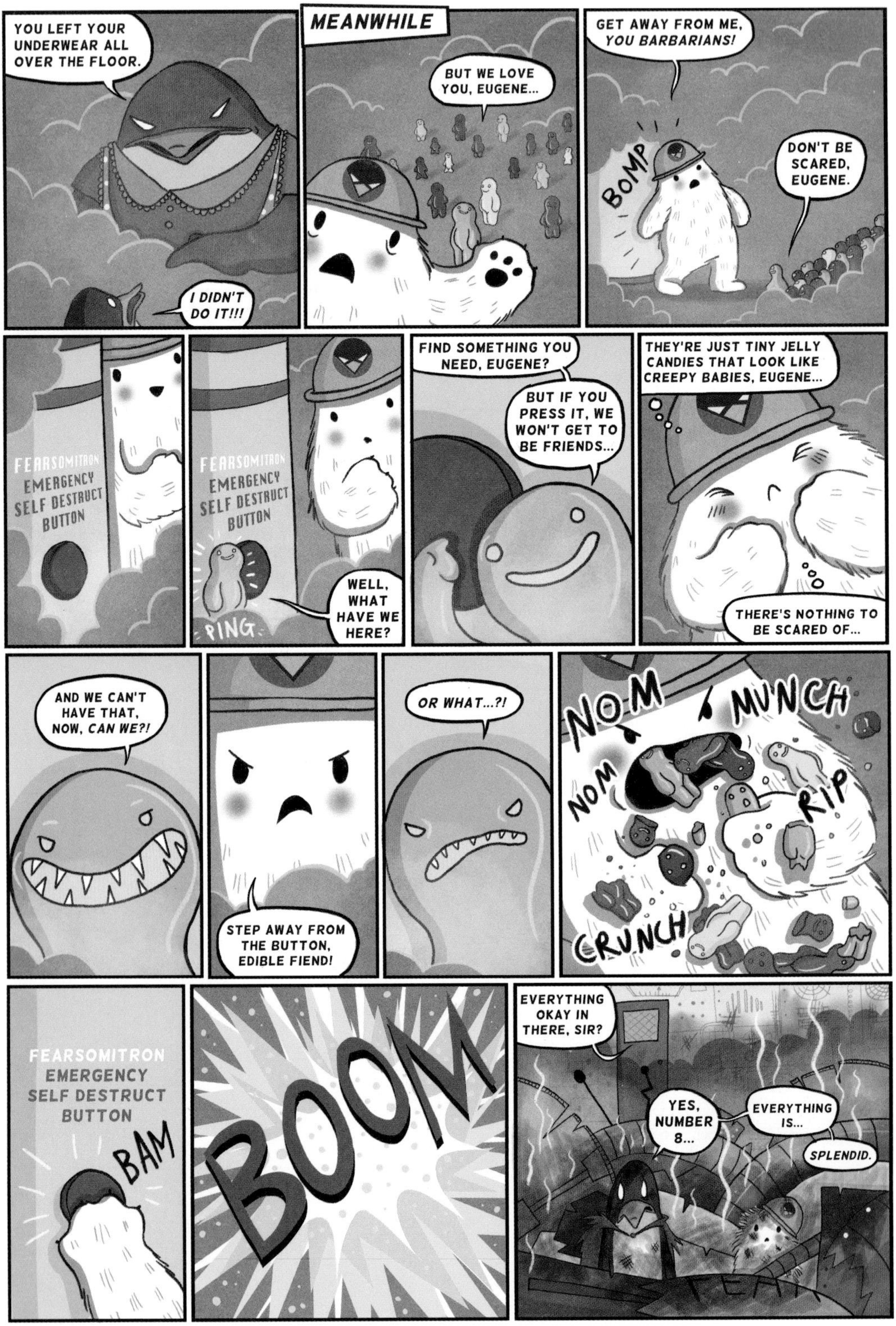

YOU LEFT YOUR UNDERWEAR ALL OVER THE FLOOR.
I DIDN'T DO IT!!!
MEANWHILE
BUT WE LOVE YOU, EUGENE...
GET AWAY FROM ME, YOU BARBARIANS!
BOMP
DON'T BE SCARED, EUGENE.
FEARSOMITRON EMERGENCY SELF DESTRUCT BUTTON
FEARSOMITRON EMERGENCY SELF DESTRUCT BUTTON
PING
WELL, WHAT HAVE WE HERE?
FIND SOMETHING YOU NEED, EUGENE?
BUT IF YOU PRESS IT, WE WON'T GET TO BE FRIENDS...
THEY'RE JUST TINY JELLY CANDIES THAT LOOK LIKE CREEPY BABIES, EUGENE...
THERE'S NOTHING TO BE SCARED OF...
AND WE CAN'T HAVE THAT, NOW, CAN WE?!
STEP AWAY FROM THE BUTTON, EDIBLE FIEND!
OR WHAT...?!
NOM
MUNCH
NOM
RIP
CRUNCH
FEARSOMITRON EMERGENCY SELF DESTRUCT BUTTON
BAM
BOOM
EVERYTHING OKAY IN THERE, SIR?
YES, NUMBER 8...
EVERYTHING IS...
SPLENDID.

CAT-ASTROPHE

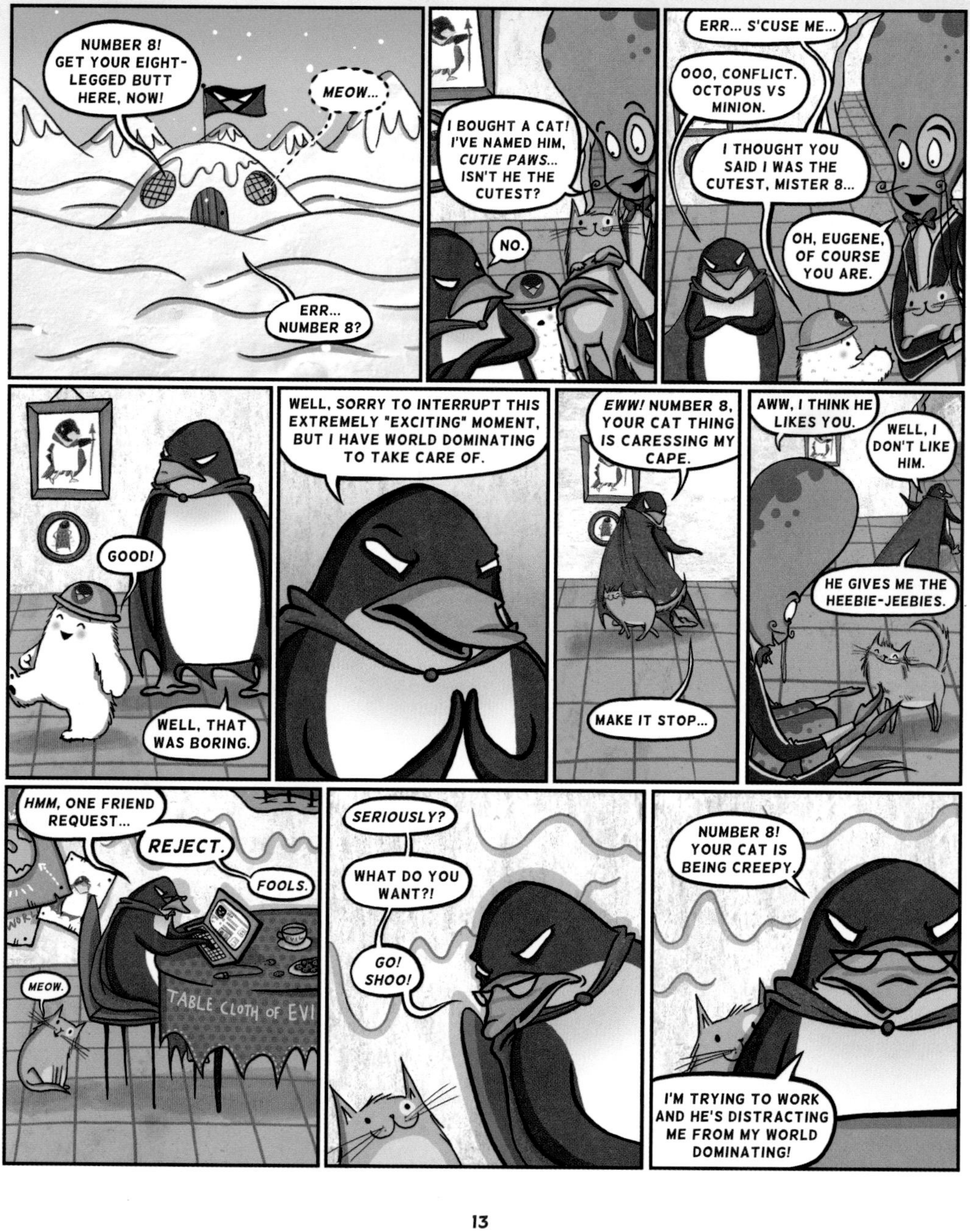
NUMBER 8! GET YOUR EIGHT-LEGGED BUTT HERE, NOW!
MEOW...
ERR... NUMBER 8?
I BOUGHT A CAT! I'VE NAMED HIM, CUTIE PAWS... ISN'T HE THE CUTEST?
NO.
ERR... S'CUSE ME...
OOO, CONFLICT. OCTOPUS VS MINION.
I THOUGHT YOU SAID I WAS THE CUTEST, MISTER 8...
OH, EUGENE, OF COURSE YOU ARE.
GOOD!
WELL, THAT WAS BORING.
WELL, SORRY TO INTERRUPT THIS EXTREMELY "EXCITING" MOMENT, BUT I HAVE WORLD DOMINATING TO TAKE CARE OF.
EWW! NUMBER 8, YOUR CAT THING IS CARESSING MY CAPE.
MAKE IT STOP...
AWW, I THINK HE LIKES YOU.
WELL, I DON'T LIKE HIM.
HE GIVES ME THE HEEBIE-JEEBIES.
HMM, ONE FRIEND REQUEST...
REJECT.
FOOLS.
MEOW.
TABLE CLOTH OF EVI
SERIOUSLY?
WHAT DO YOU WANT?!
GO! SHOO!
NUMBER 8! YOUR CAT IS BEING CREEPY.
I'M TRYING TO WORK AND HE'S DISTRACTING ME FROM MY WORLD DOMINATING!

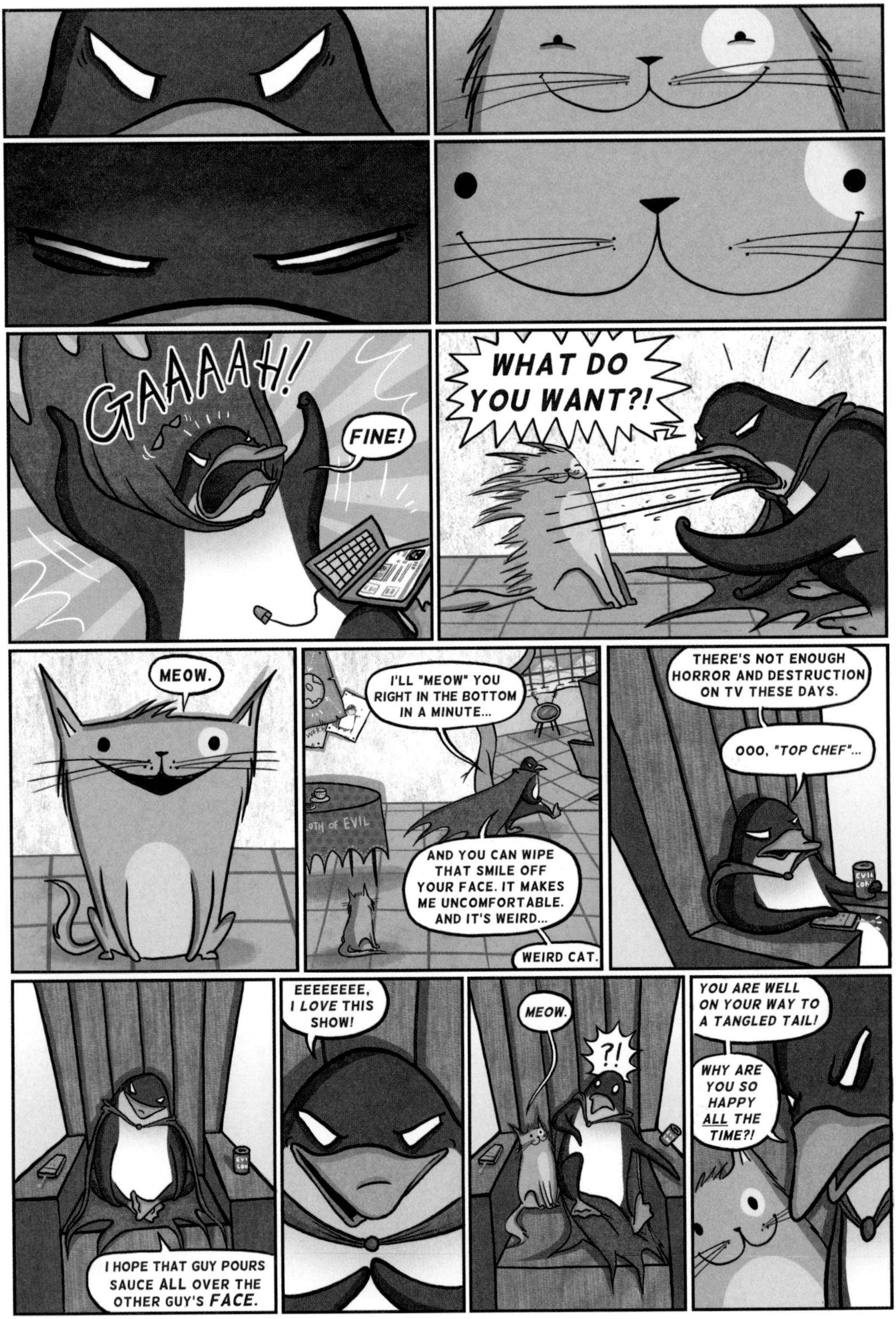
GAAAAH!
FINE!
WHAT DO YOU WANT?!
MEOW.
I'LL "MEOW" YOU RIGHT IN THE BOTTOM IN A MINUTE...
AND YOU CAN WIPE THAT SMILE OFF YOUR FACE. IT MAKES ME UNCOMFORTABLE. AND IT'S WEIRD...
WEIRD CAT.
THERE'S NOT ENOUGH HORROR AND DESTRUCTION ON TV THESE DAYS.
OOO, "TOP CHEF"...
I HOPE THAT GUY POURS SAUCE ALL OVER THE OTHER GUY'S FACE.
EEEEEEEE, I LOVE THIS SHOW!
MEOW.
?!
YOU ARE WELL ON YOUR WAY TO A TANGLED TAIL!
WHY ARE YOU SO HAPPY ALL THE TIME?!

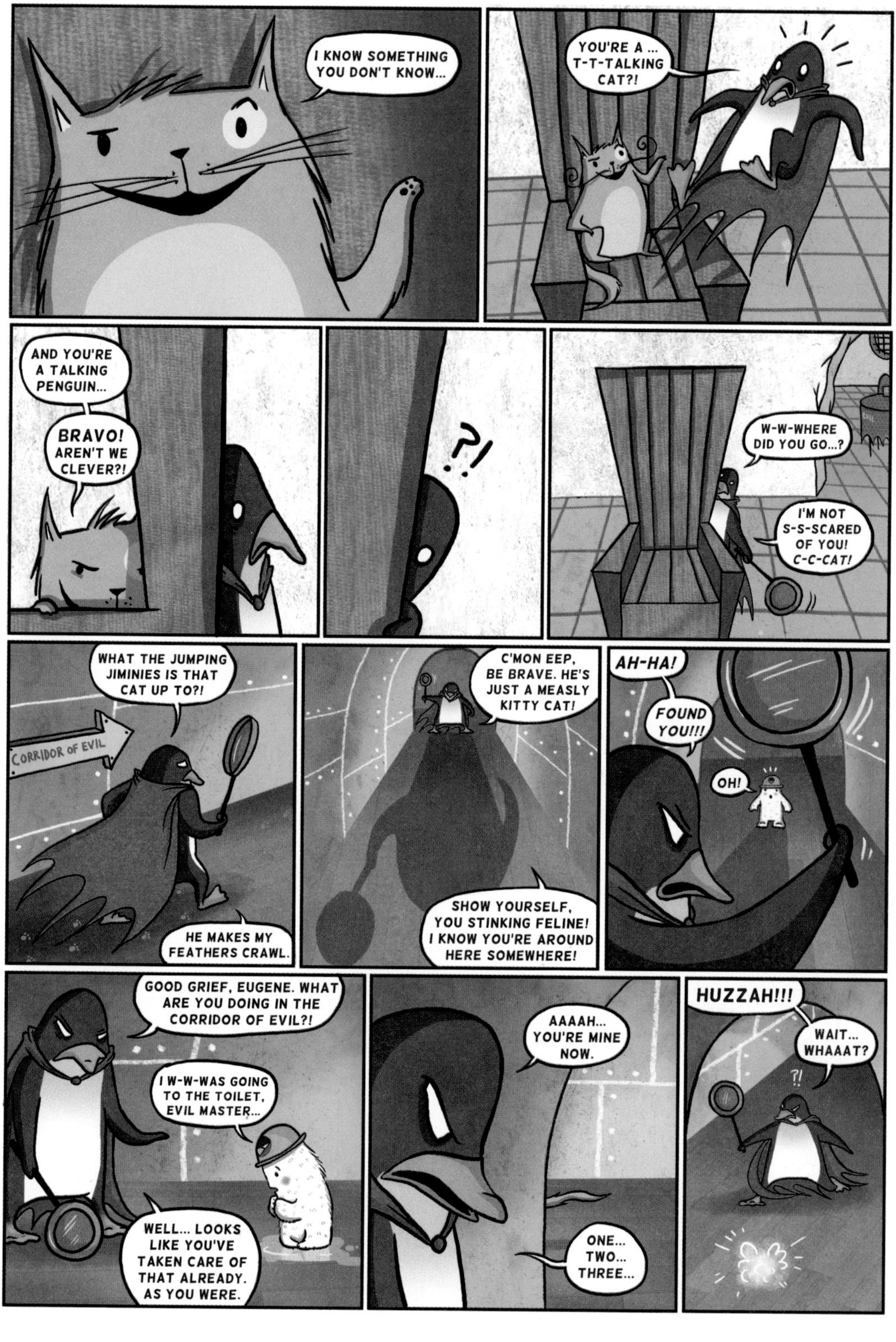

I KNOW SOMETHING YOU DON'T KNOW...
YOU'RE A ... T-T-TALKING CAT?!
AND YOU'RE A TALKING PENGUIN...
BRAVO! AREN'T WE CLEVER?!
?!
W-W-WHERE DID YOU GO...?
I'M NOT S-S-SCARED OF YOU! C-C-CAT!
WHAT THE JUMPING JIMINIES IS THAT CAT UP TO?!
CORRIDOR OF EVIL
HE MAKES MY FEATHERS CRAWL.
C'MON EEP, BE BRAVE. HE'S JUST A MEASLY KITTY CAT!
SHOW YOURSELF, YOU STINKING FELINE! I KNOW YOU'RE AROUND HERE SOMEWHERE!
AH-HA!
FOUND YOU!!!
OH!
GOOD GRIEF, EUGENE. WHAT ARE YOU DOING IN THE CORRIDOR OF EVIL?!
I W-W-WAS GOING TO THE TOILET, EVIL MASTER...
WELL... LOOKS LIKE YOU'VE TAKEN CARE OF THAT ALREADY. AS YOU WERE.
AAAAH... YOU'RE MINE NOW.
ONE... TWO... THREE...
HUZZAH!!!
WAIT... WHAAAT?
?!

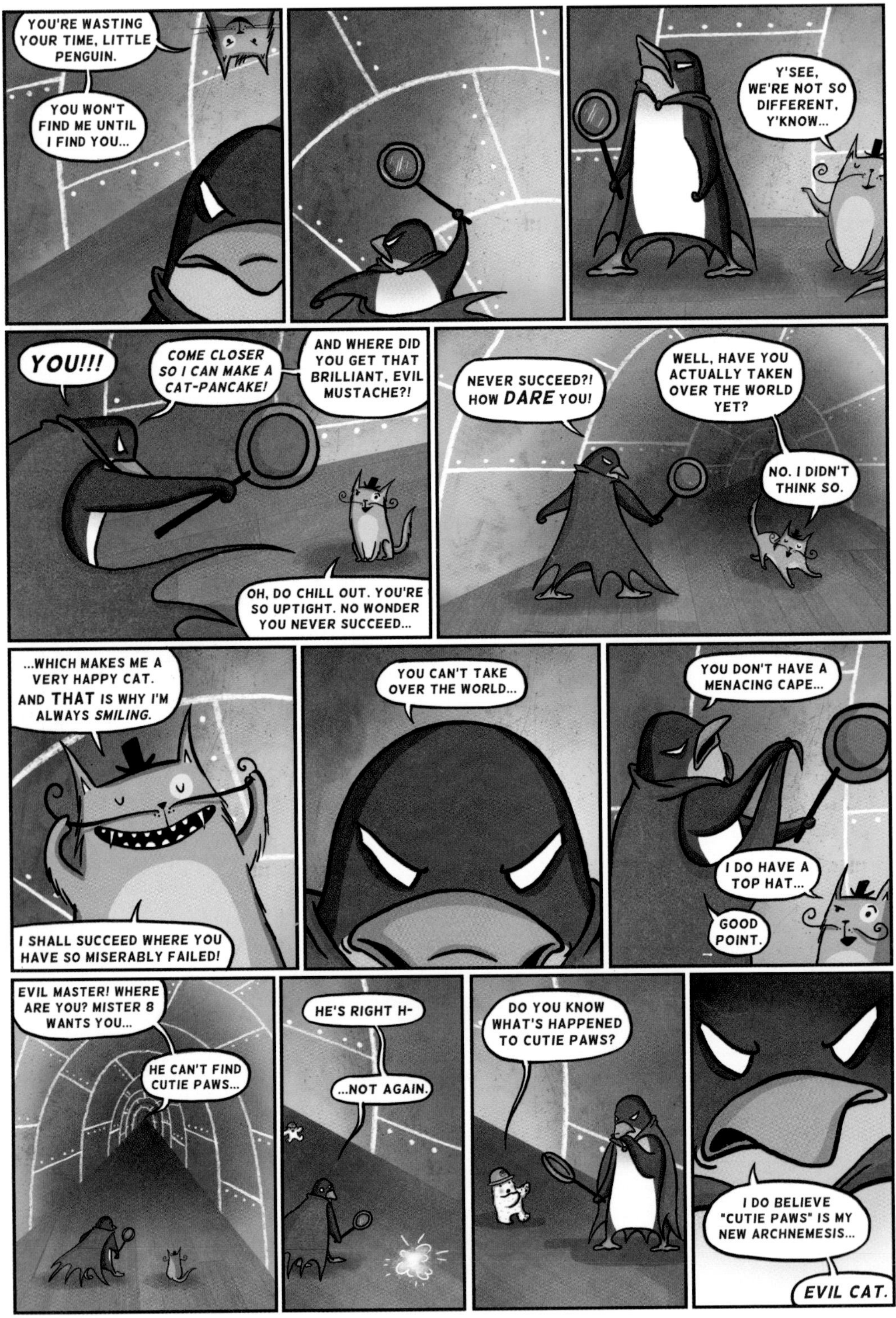
YOU'RE WASTING YOUR TIME, LITTLE PENGUIN.
YOU WON'T FIND ME UNTIL I FIND YOU...
Y'SEE, WE'RE NOT SO DIFFERENT, Y'KNOW...
YOU!!!
COME CLOSER SO I CAN MAKE A CAT-PANCAKE!
AND WHERE DID YOU GET THAT BRILLIANT, EVIL MUSTACHE?!
OH, DO CHILL OUT. YOU'RE SO UPTIGHT. NO WONDER YOU NEVER SUCCEED...
NEVER SUCCEED?! HOW DARE YOU!
WELL, HAVE YOU ACTUALLY TAKEN OVER THE WORLD YET?
NO. I DIDN'T THINK SO.
...WHICH MAKES ME A VERY HAPPY CAT. AND THAT IS WHY I'M ALWAYS SMILING.
I SHALL SUCCEED WHERE YOU HAVE SO MISERABLY FAILED!
YOU CAN'T TAKE OVER THE WORLD...
YOU DON'T HAVE A MENACING CAPE...
I DO HAVE A TOP HAT...
GOOD POINT.
EVIL MASTER! WHERE ARE YOU? MISTER 8 WANTS YOU...
HE CAN'T FIND CUTIE PAWS...
HE'S RIGHT H-
...NOT AGAIN.
DO YOU KNOW WHAT'S HAPPENED TO CUTIE PAWS?
I DO BELIEVE "CUTIE PAWS" IS MY NEW ARCHNEMESIS...
EVIL CAT.

WORLD WIDE WEB

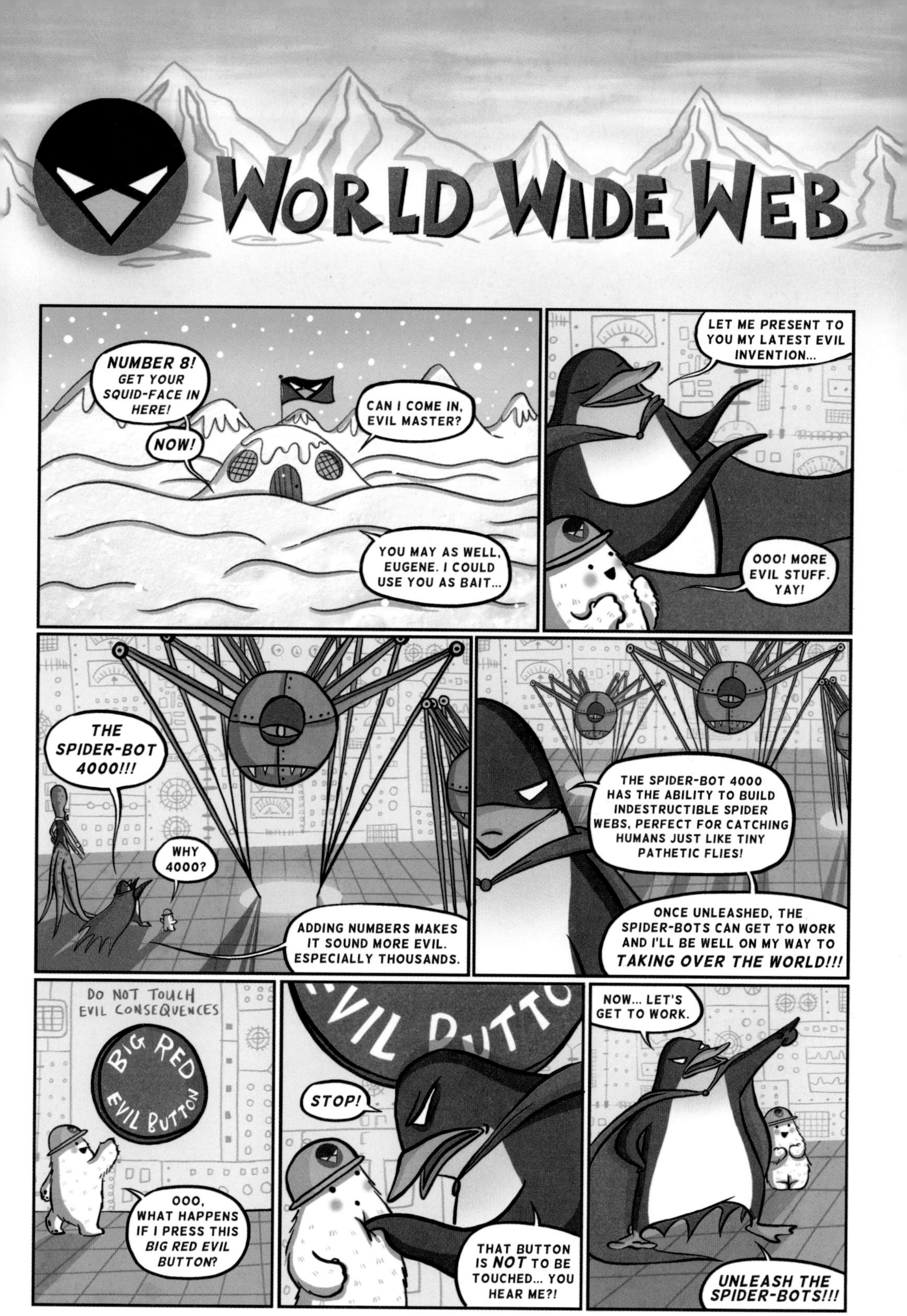

NUMBER 8! GET YOUR SQUID-FACE IN HERE!
NOW!
CAN I COME IN, EVIL MASTER?
YOU MAY AS WELL, EUGENE. I COULD USE YOU AS BAIT...
LET ME PRESENT TO YOU MY LATEST EVIL INVENTION...
OOO! MORE EVIL STUFF. YAY!
THE SPIDER-BOT 4000!!!
WHY 4000?
ADDING NUMBERS MAKES IT SOUND MORE EVIL. ESPECIALLY THOUSANDS.
THE SPIDER-BOT 4000 HAS THE ABILITY TO BUILD INDESTRUCTIBLE SPIDER WEBS, PERFECT FOR CATCHING HUMANS JUST LIKE TINY PATHETIC FLIES!
ONCE UNLEASHED, THE SPIDER-BOTS CAN GET TO WORK AND I'LL BE WELL ON MY WAY TO TAKING OVER THE WORLD!!!
DO NOT TOUCH
EVIL CONSEQUENCES
BIG RED EVIL BUTTON
OOO, WHAT HAPPENS IF I PRESS THIS BIG RED EVIL BUTTON?
STOP!
THAT BUTTON IS NOT TO BE TOUCHED... YOU HEAR ME?!
NOW... LET'S GET TO WORK.
UNLEASH THE SPIDER-BOTS!!!

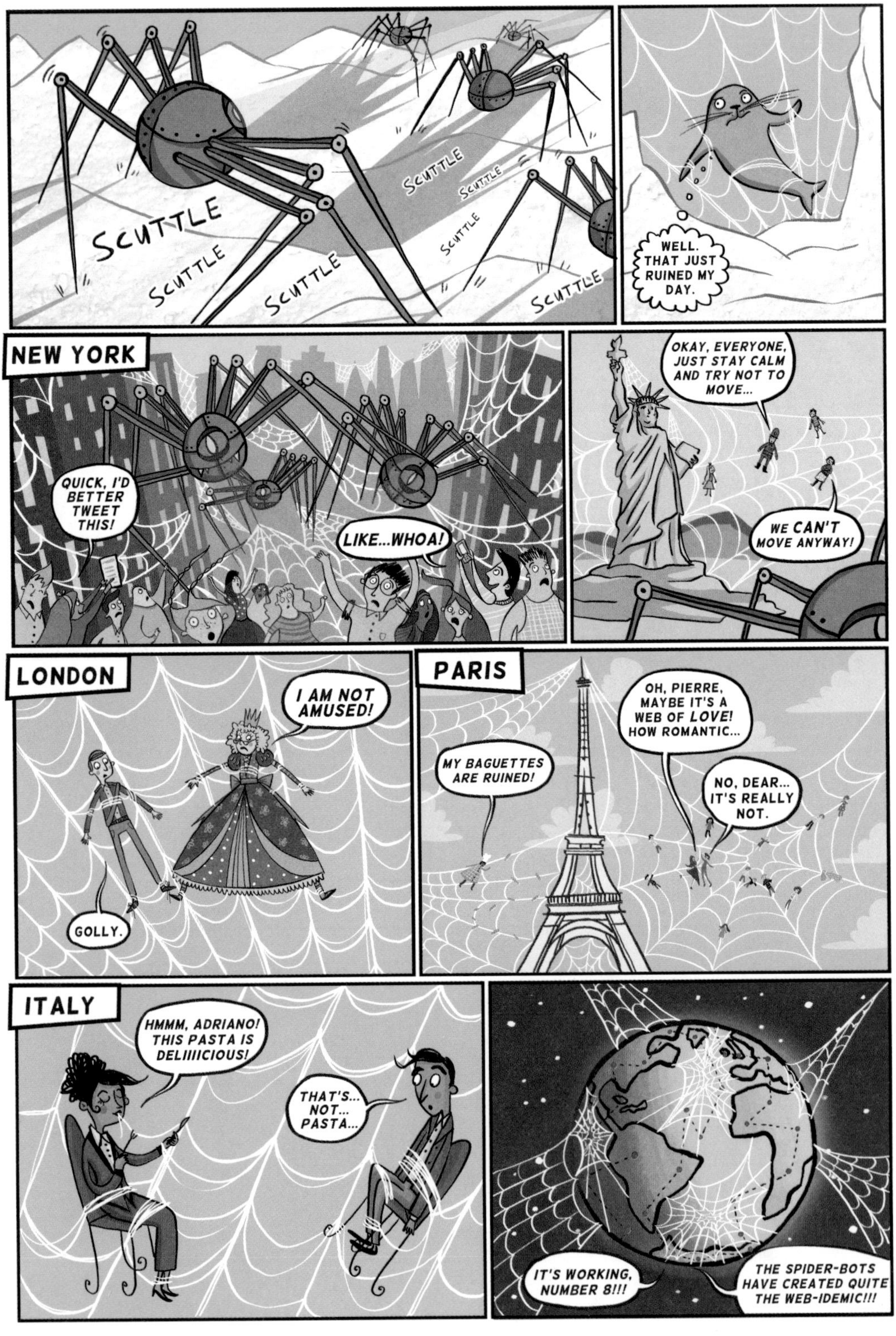
SCUTTLE
SCUTTLE
SCUTTLE
SCUTTLE
SCUTTLE
SCUTTLE
SCUTTLE
WELL. THAT JUST RUINED MY DAY.
NEW YORK
QUICK, I'D BETTER TWEET THIS!
LIKE...WHOA!
OKAY, EVERYONE, JUST STAY CALM AND TRY NOT TO MOVE...
WE CAN'T MOVE ANYWAY!
LONDON
I AM NOT AMUSED!
GOLLY.
PARIS
OH, PIERRE, MAYBE IT'S A WEB OF LOVE! HOW ROMANTIC...
MY BAGUETTES ARE RUINED!
NO, DEAR... IT'S REALLY NOT.
ITALY
HMMM, ADRIANO! THIS PASTA IS DELIIIICIOUS!
THAT'S... NOT... PASTA...
IT'S WORKING, NUMBER 8!!!
THE SPIDER-BOTS HAVE CREATED QUITE THE WEB-IDEMIC!!!

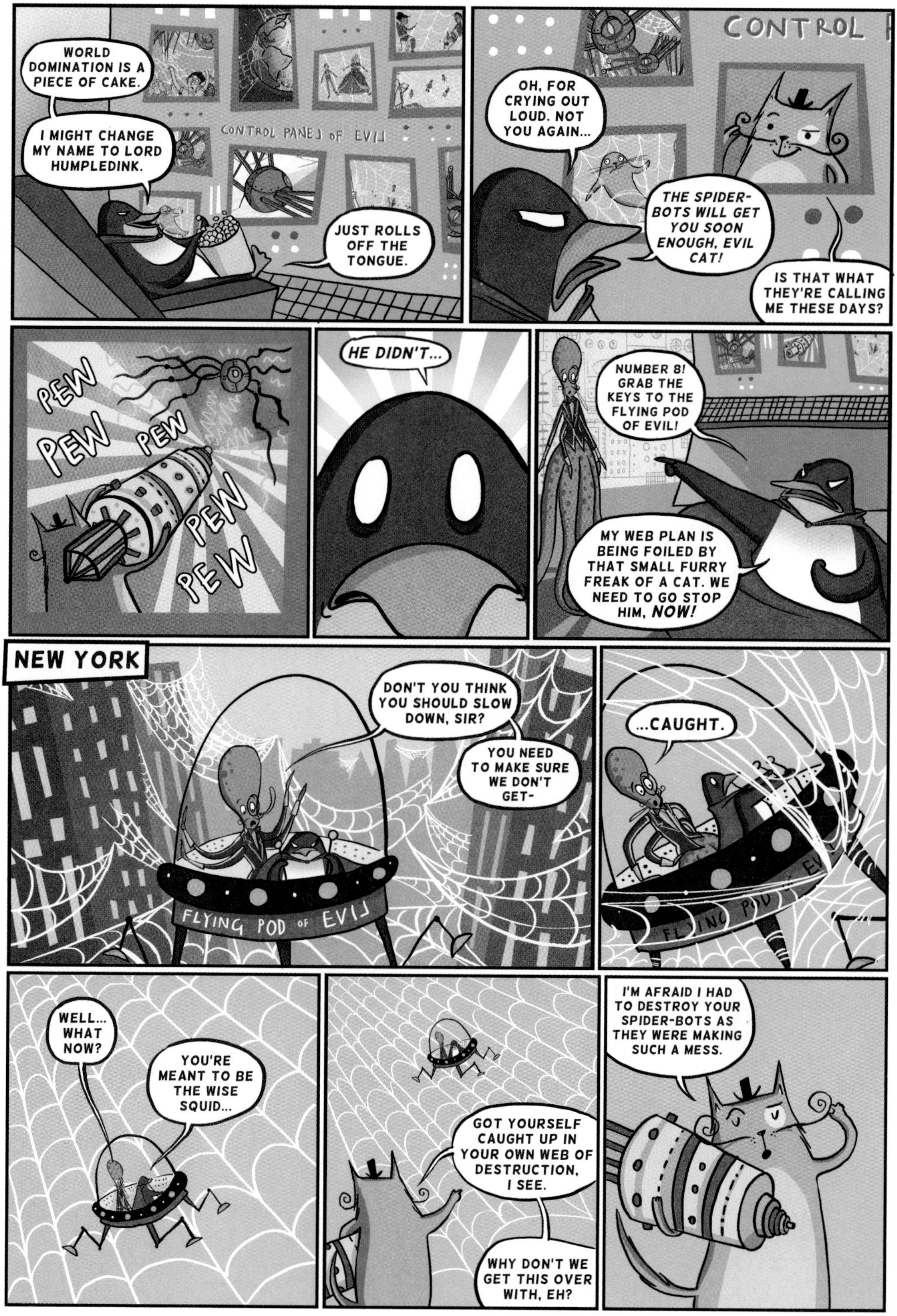
WORLD DOMINATION IS A PIECE OF CAKE.
I MIGHT CHANGE MY NAME TO LORD HUMPLEDINK.
CONTROL PANEL OF EVIL
JUST ROLLS OFF THE TONGUE.
CONTROL
OH, FOR CRYING OUT LOUD. NOT YOU AGAIN...
THE SPIDER-BOTS WILL GET YOU SOON ENOUGH, EVIL CAT!
IS THAT WHAT THEY'RE CALLING ME THESE DAYS?
PEW
PEW
PEW
PEW
PEW
HE DIDN'T...
NUMBER 8! GRAB THE KEYS TO THE FLYING POD OF EVIL!
MY WEB PLAN IS BEING FOILED BY THAT SMALL FURRY FREAK OF A CAT. WE NEED TO GO STOP HIM, NOW!
NEW YORK
DON'T YOU THINK YOU SHOULD SLOW DOWN, SIR?
YOU NEED TO MAKE SURE WE DON'T GET-
FLYING POD OF EVIL
...CAUGHT.
WELL... WHAT NOW?
YOU'RE MEANT TO BE THE WISE SQUID...
GOT YOURSELF CAUGHT UP IN YOUR OWN WEB OF DESTRUCTION, I SEE.
WHY DON'T WE GET THIS OVER WITH, EH?
I'M AFRAID I HAD TO DESTROY YOUR SPIDER-BOTS AS THEY WERE MAKING SUCH A MESS.

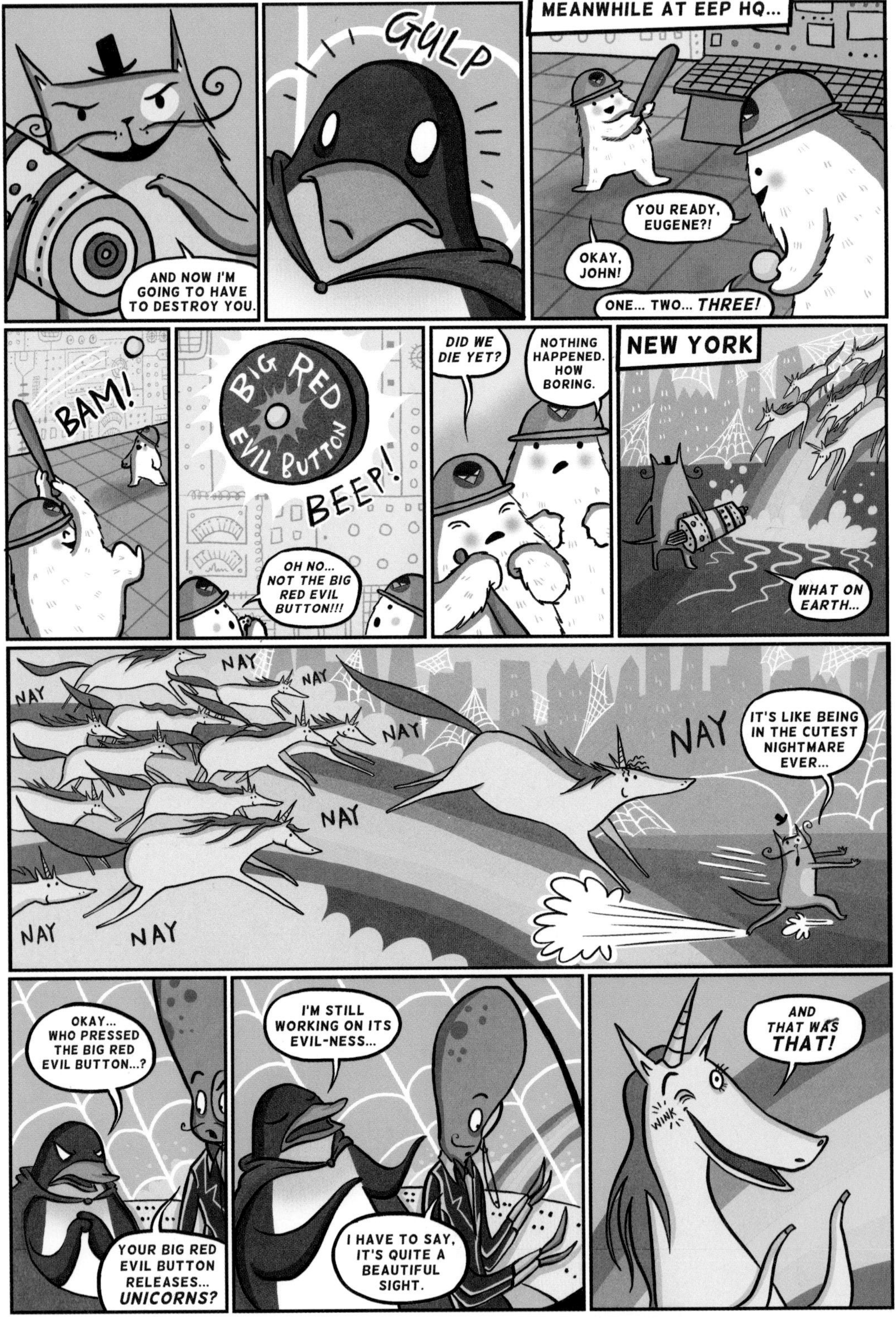
AND NOW I'M GOING TO HAVE TO DESTROY YOU.
GULP
MEANWHILE AT EEP HQ...
YOU READY, EUGENE?!
OKAY, JOHN!
ONE... TWO... THREE!
BAM!
BIG RED EVIL BUTTON
BEEP!
OH NO... NOT THE BIG RED EVIL BUTTON!!!
DID WE DIE YET?
NOTHING HAPPENED. HOW BORING.
NEW YORK
WHAT ON EARTH...
NAY
NAY
NAY
NAY
NAY
NAY
NAY
NAY
IT'S LIKE BEING IN THE CUTEST NIGHTMARE EVER...
OKAY... WHO PRESSED THE BIG RED EVIL BUTTON...?
YOUR BIG RED EVIL BUTTON RELEASES... UNICORNS?
I'M STILL WORKING ON ITS EVIL-NESS...
I HAVE TO SAY, IT'S QUITE A BEAUTIFUL SIGHT.
AND THAT WAS THAT!
WINK

The Truce: Part 1

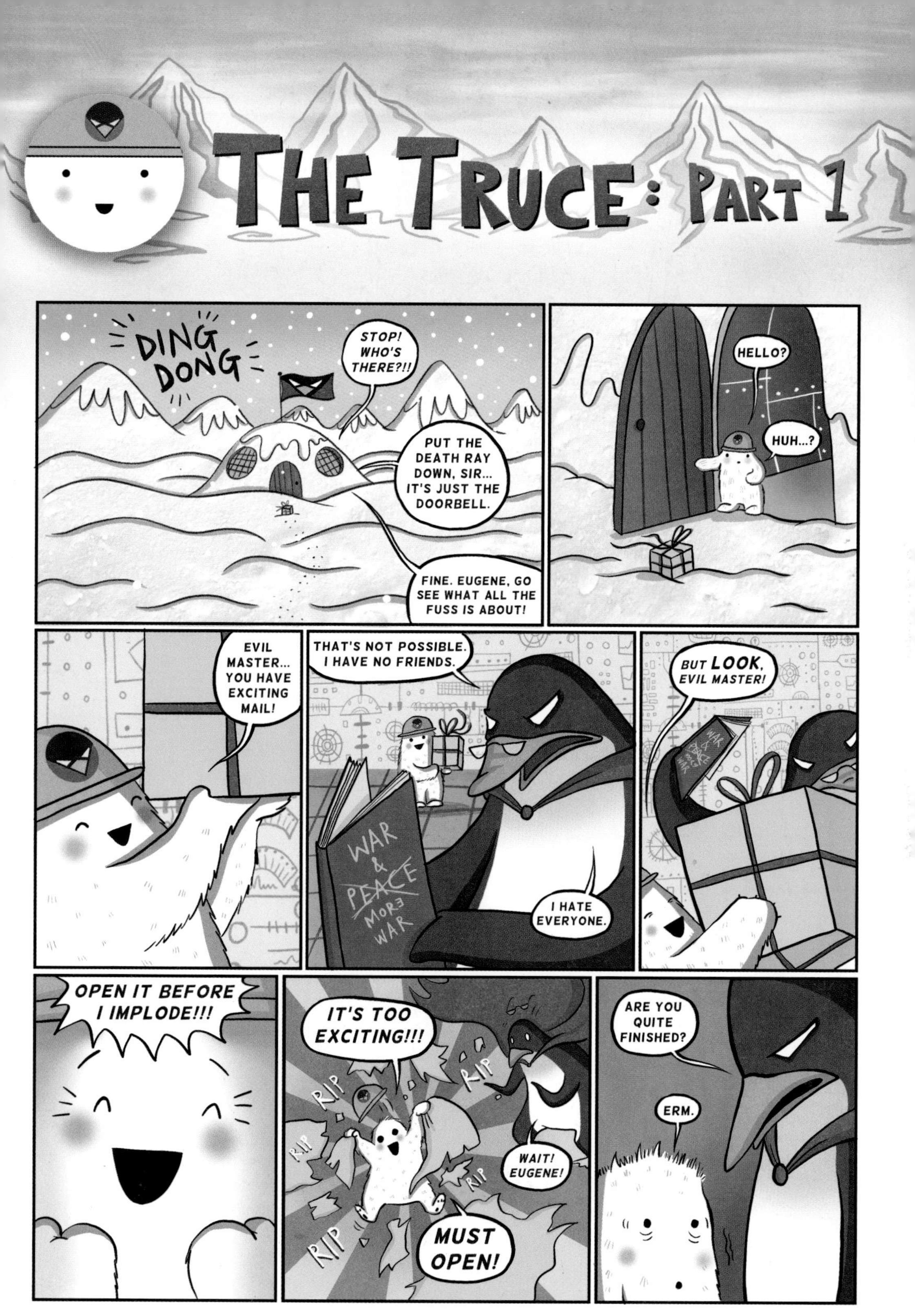
DING DONG
STOP! WHO'S THERE?!!
PUT THE DEATH RAY DOWN, SIR... IT'S JUST THE DOORBELL.
FINE. EUGENE, GO SEE WHAT ALL THE FUSS IS ABOUT!
HELLO?
HUH...?
EVIL MASTER... YOU HAVE EXCITING MAIL!
THAT'S NOT POSSIBLE. I HAVE NO FRIENDS.
WAR & PEACE MORE WAR
I HATE EVERYONE.
BUT LOOK, EVIL MASTER!
OPEN IT BEFORE I IMPLODE!!!
IT'S TOO EXCITING!!!
RIP RIP RIP RIP RIP RIP
WAIT! EUGENE!
MUST OPEN!
ARE YOU QUITE FINISHED?
ERM.

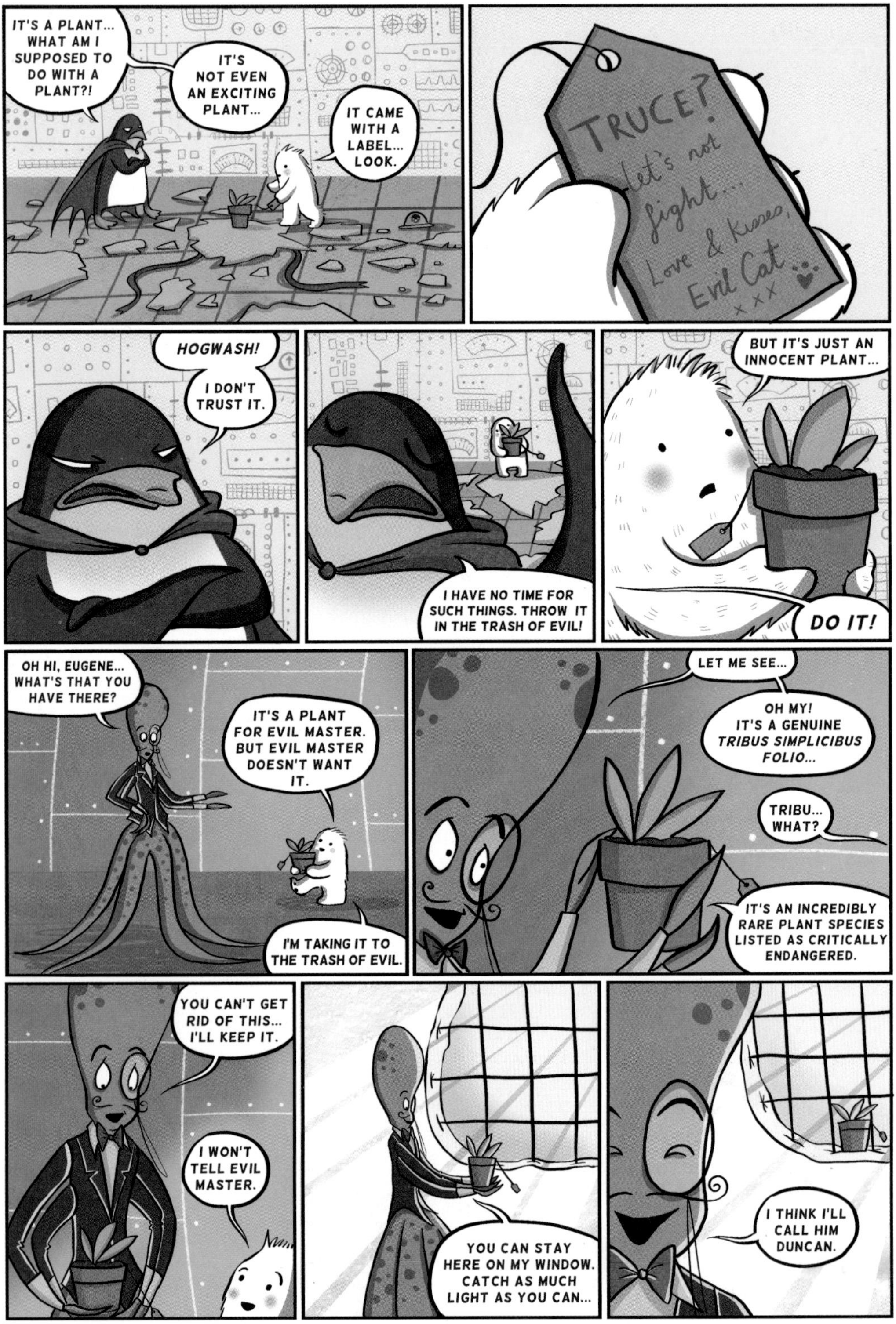
IT'S A PLANT... WHAT AM I SUPPOSED TO DO WITH A PLANT?!
IT'S NOT EVEN AN EXCITING PLANT...
IT CAME WITH A LABEL... LOOK.
TRUCE? let's not fight... Love & Kisses, Evil Cat xxx
HOGWASH!
I DON'T TRUST IT.
I HAVE NO TIME FOR SUCH THINGS. THROW IT IN THE TRASH OF EVIL!
BUT IT'S JUST AN INNOCENT PLANT...
DO IT!
OH HI, EUGENE... WHAT'S THAT YOU HAVE THERE?
IT'S A PLANT FOR EVIL MASTER. BUT EVIL MASTER DOESN'T WANT IT.
I'M TAKING IT TO THE TRASH OF EVIL.
LET ME SEE...
OH MY! IT'S A GENUINE *TRIBUS SIMPLICIBUS FOLIO*...
TRIBU... WHAT?
IT'S AN INCREDIBLY RARE PLANT SPECIES LISTED AS CRITICALLY ENDANGERED.
YOU CAN'T GET RID OF THIS... I'LL KEEP IT.
I WON'T TELL EVIL MASTER.
YOU CAN STAY HERE ON MY WINDOW. CATCH AS MUCH LIGHT AS YOU CAN...
I THINK I'LL CALL HIM DUNCAN.

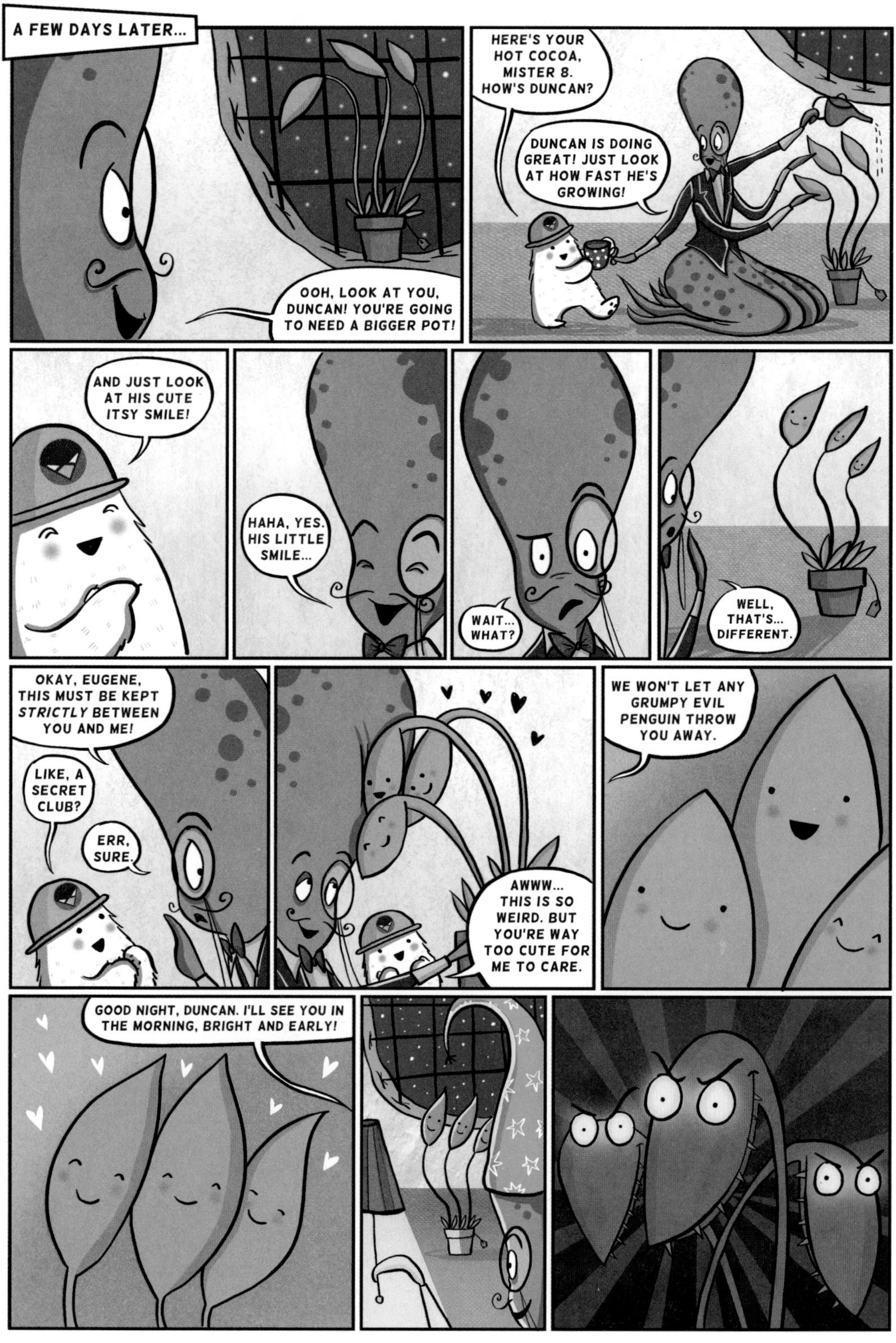
A FEW DAYS LATER...
OOH, LOOK AT YOU, DUNCAN! YOU'RE GOING TO NEED A BIGGER POT!
HERE'S YOUR HOT COCOA, MISTER 8. HOW'S DUNCAN?
DUNCAN IS DOING GREAT! JUST LOOK AT HOW FAST HE'S GROWING!
AND JUST LOOK AT HIS CUTE ITSY SMILE!
HAHA, YES. HIS LITTLE SMILE...
WAIT... WHAT?
WELL, THAT'S... DIFFERENT.
OKAY, EUGENE, THIS MUST BE KEPT STRICTLY BETWEEN YOU AND ME!
LIKE, A SECRET CLUB?
ERR, SURE.
AWWW... THIS IS SO WEIRD. BUT YOU'RE WAY TOO CUTE FOR ME TO CARE.
WE WON'T LET ANY GRUMPY EVIL PENGUIN THROW YOU AWAY.
GOOD NIGHT, DUNCAN. I'LL SEE YOU IN THE MORNING, BRIGHT AND EARLY!

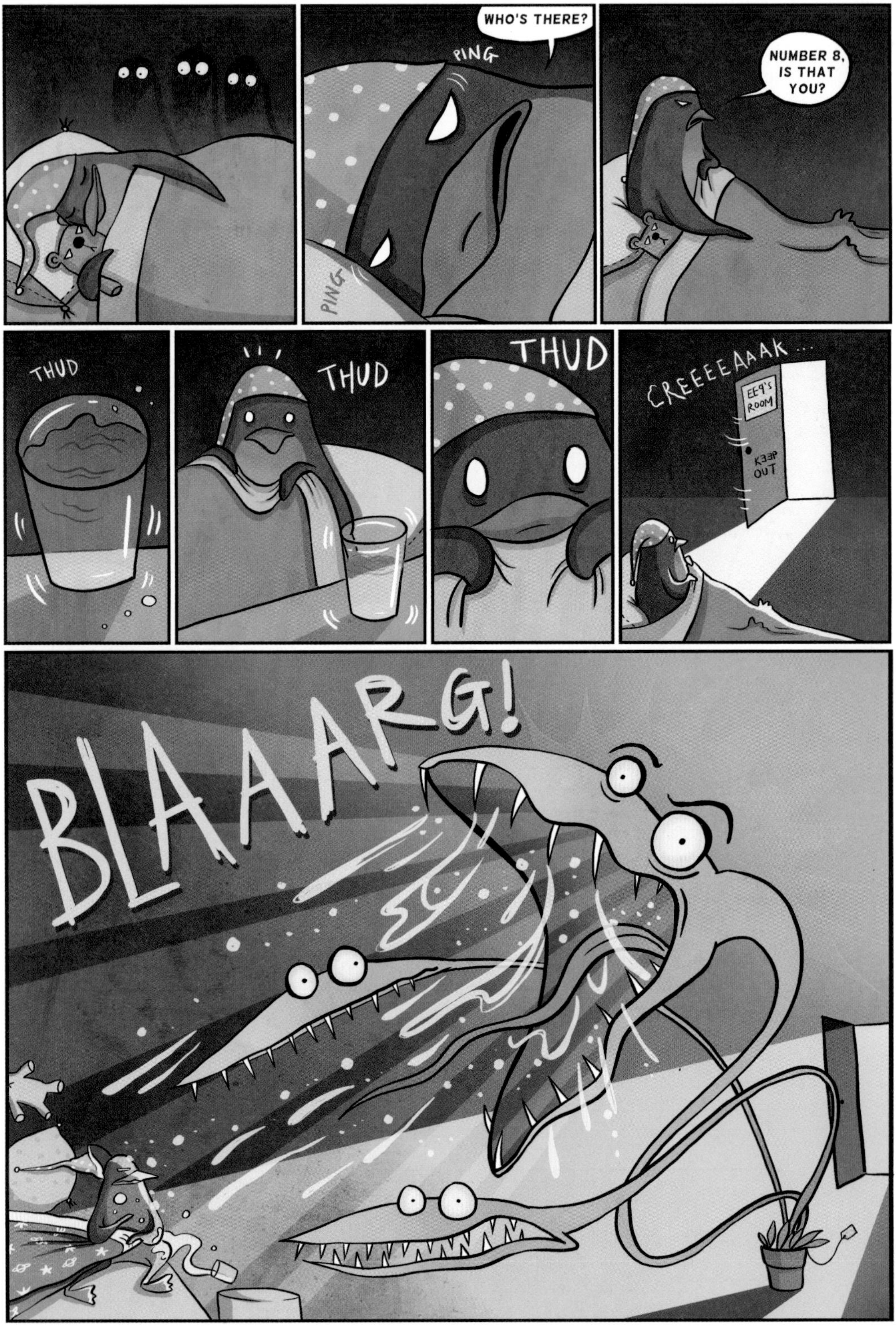
WHO'S THERE?
PING
PING
NUMBER 8, IS THAT YOU?
THUD
THUD
THUD
CREEEEAAAK...
EEG'S ROOM
KEEP OUT
BLAAARG!

PREVIOUSLY ON EEP...

THIS GUY...

SENT THIS GIFT...

TO THIS GUY...

BUT IT TURNED INTO THIS.

AND NOW THIS IS HAPPENING.

FLARG!

BLAAH!

RAAAAH!

NUMBER 8!!!

CORRIDOR OF EVIL

GAAAAAH!

OH MY!

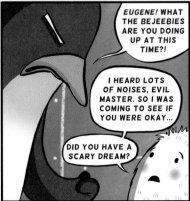

EUGENE! WHAT THE BEJEEBIES ARE YOU DOING UP AT THIS TIME?!

I HEARD LOTS OF NOISES, EVIL MASTER. SO I WAS COMING TO SEE IF YOU WERE OKAY...

DID YOU HAVE A SCARY DREAM?

THERE'S A BIG WIGGLY MONSTER PLANT THING IN MY BEDROOM OF EVIL!

EXPLAIN THAT!

OH, THAT DOESN'T SOUND PLEASANT.

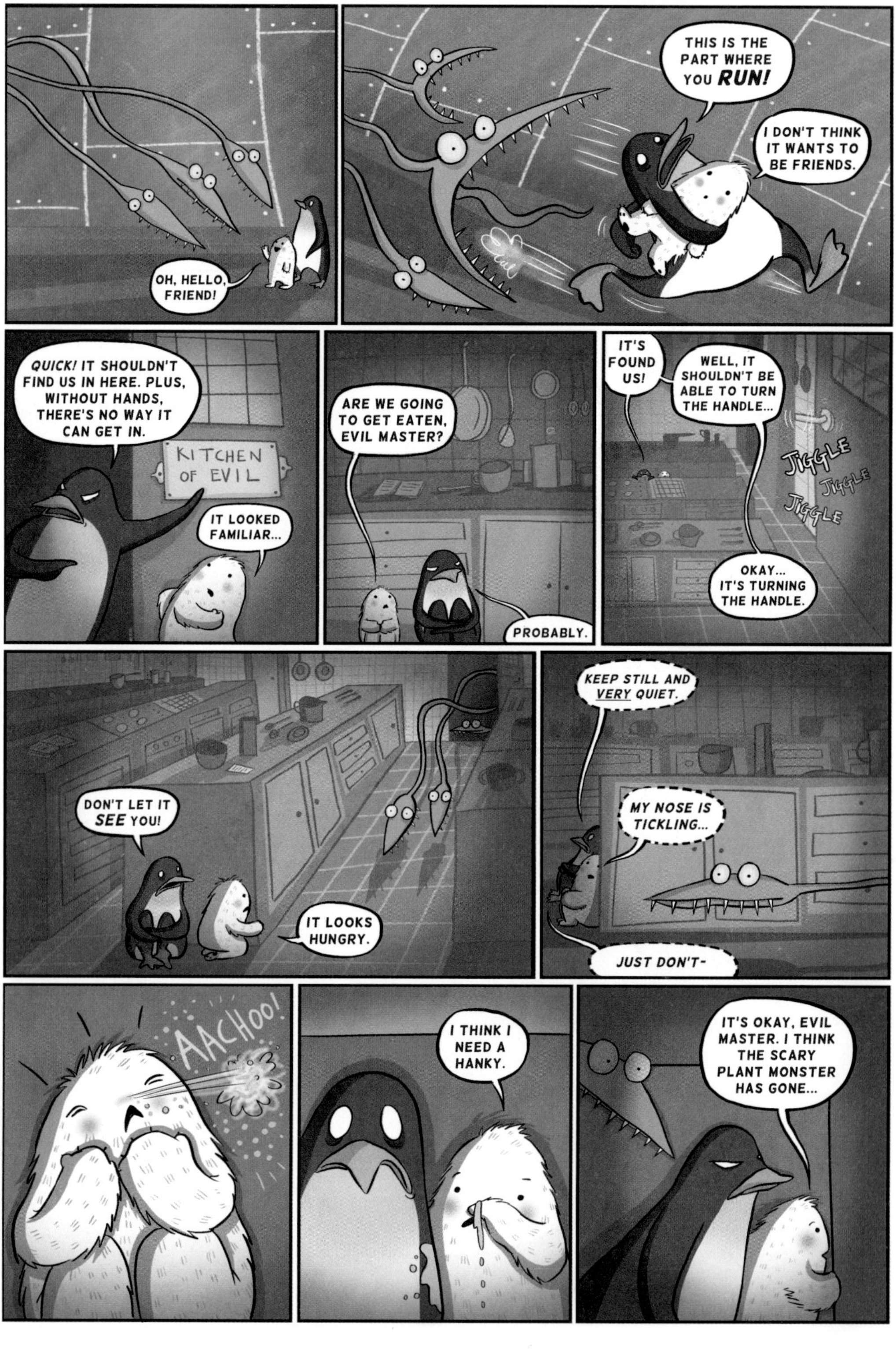
OH, HELLO, FRIEND!
THIS IS THE PART WHERE YOU **RUN!**
I DON'T THINK IT WANTS TO BE FRIENDS.
QUICK! IT SHOULDN'T FIND US IN HERE. PLUS, WITHOUT HANDS, THERE'S NO WAY IT CAN GET IN.
KITCHEN OF EVIL
IT LOOKED FAMILIAR...
ARE WE GOING TO GET EATEN, EVIL MASTER?
PROBABLY.
IT'S FOUND US!
WELL, IT SHOULDN'T BE ABLE TO TURN THE HANDLE...
JIGGLE
JIGGLE
JIGGLE
OKAY... IT'S TURNING THE HANDLE.
DON'T LET IT **SEE** YOU!
IT LOOKS HUNGRY.
KEEP STILL AND VERY QUIET.
MY NOSE IS TICKLING...
JUST DON'T-
AACHOO!
I THINK I NEED A HANKY.
IT'S OKAY, EVIL MASTER. I THINK THE SCARY PLANT MONSTER HAS GONE...

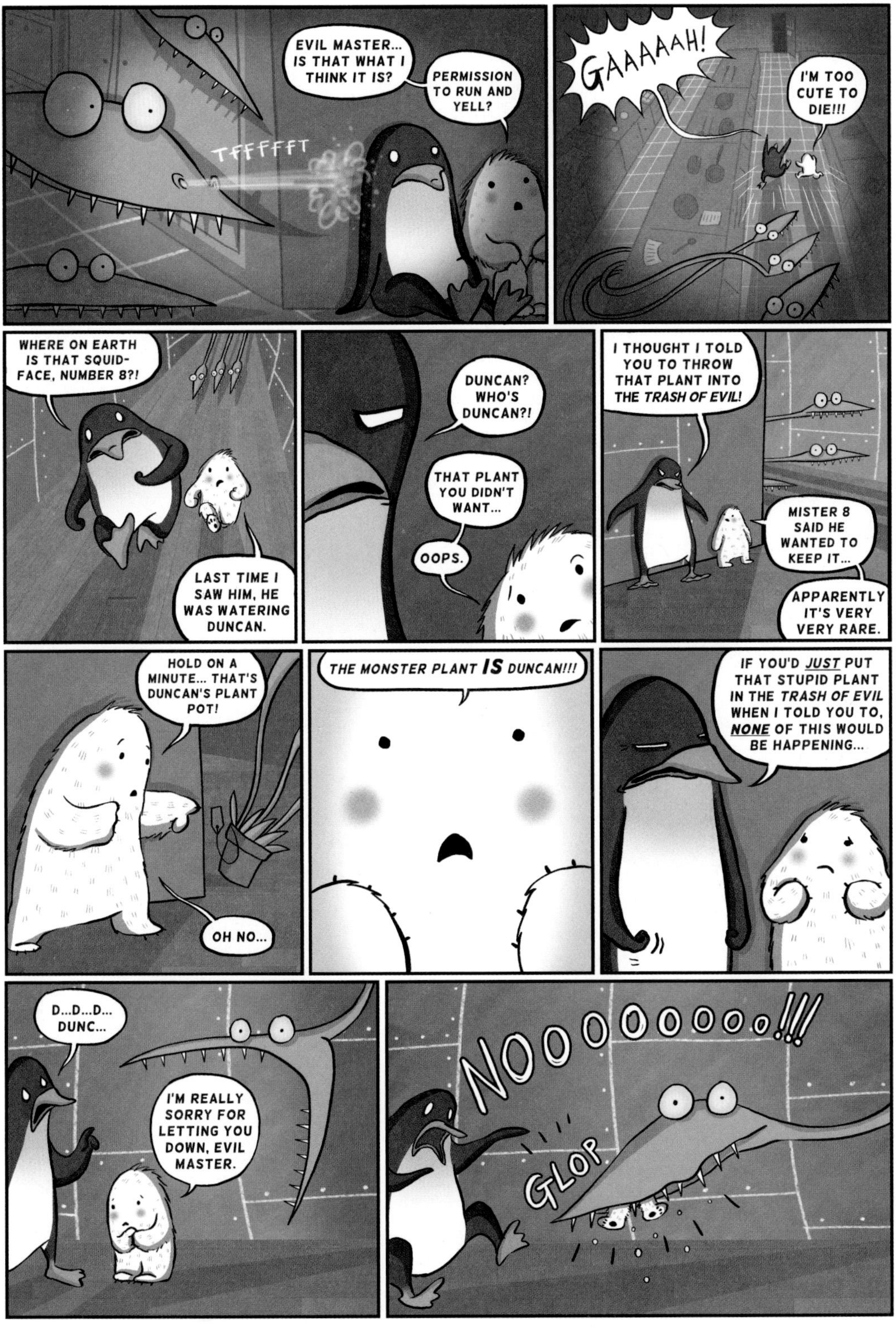
EVIL MASTER... IS THAT WHAT I THINK IT IS?
PERMISSION TO RUN AND YELL?
TFFFFFT
GAAAAAH!
I'M TOO CUTE TO DIE!!!
WHERE ON EARTH IS THAT SQUID-FACE, NUMBER 8?!
LAST TIME I SAW HIM, HE WAS WATERING DUNCAN.
DUNCAN? WHO'S DUNCAN?!
THAT PLANT YOU DIDN'T WANT...
OOPS.
I THOUGHT I TOLD YOU TO THROW THAT PLANT INTO THE *TRASH OF EVIL!*
MISTER 8 SAID HE WANTED TO KEEP IT...
APPARENTLY IT'S VERY VERY RARE.
HOLD ON A MINUTE... THAT'S DUNCAN'S PLANT POT!
OH NO...
THE MONSTER PLANT **IS** *DUNCAN!!!*
IF YOU'D *JUST* PUT THAT STUPID PLANT IN THE *TRASH OF EVIL* WHEN I TOLD YOU TO, *NONE* OF THIS WOULD BE HAPPENING...
D...D...D... DUNC...
I'M REALLY SORRY FOR LETTING YOU DOWN, EVIL MASTER.
NOOOOOOOOO!!!
GLOP

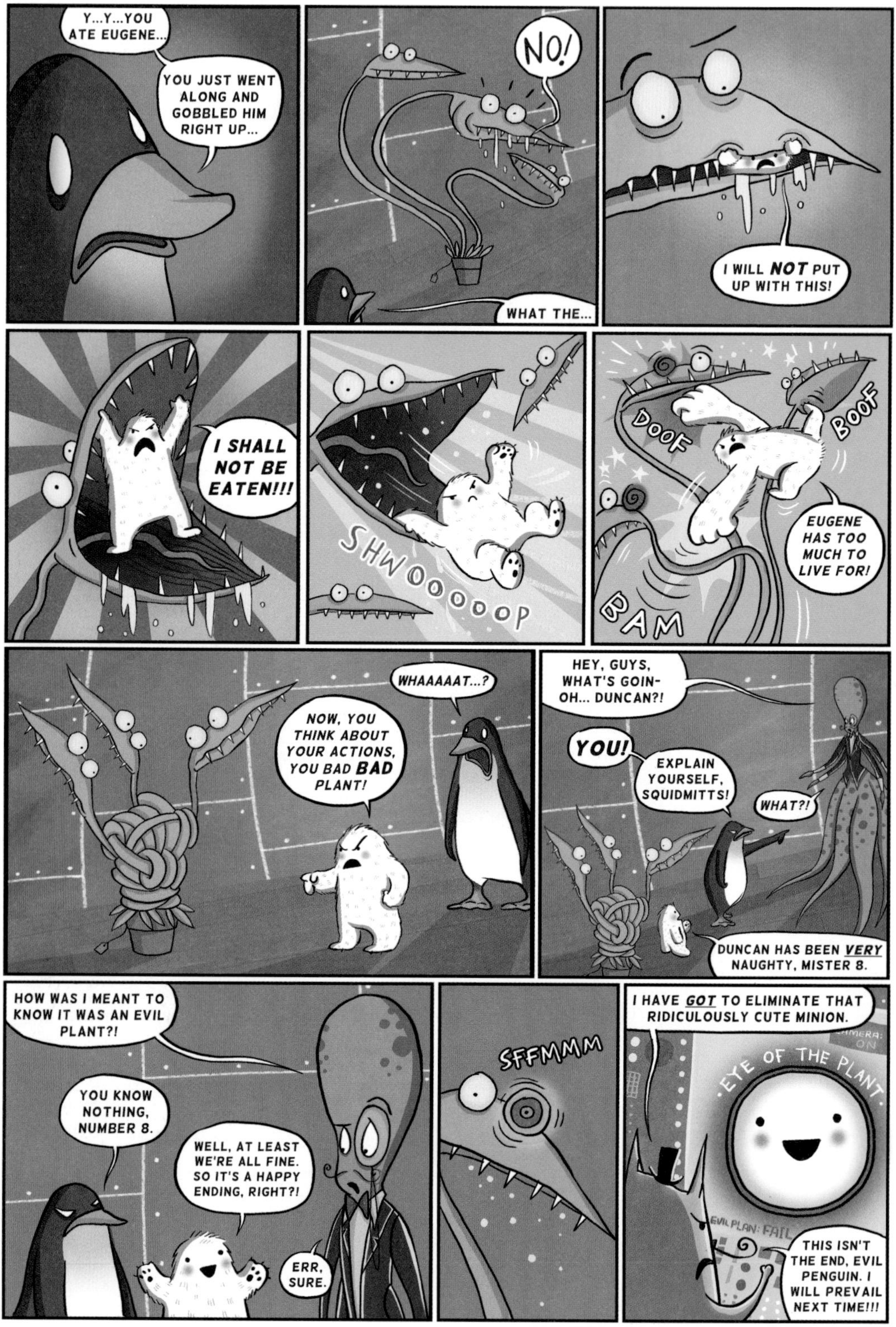

Y...Y...YOU ATE EUGENE...
YOU JUST WENT ALONG AND GOBBLED HIM RIGHT UP...
NO!
WHAT THE...
I WILL **NOT** PUT UP WITH THIS!
I SHALL NOT BE EATEN!!!
SHWOOOOOOP
DOOF
BOOF
EUGENE HAS TOO MUCH TO LIVE FOR!
BAM
WHAAAAAT...?
NOW, YOU THINK ABOUT YOUR ACTIONS, YOU BAD **BAD** PLANT!
HEY, GUYS, WHAT'S GOIN- OH... DUNCAN?!
YOU!
EXPLAIN YOURSELF, SQUIDMITTS!
WHAT?!
DUNCAN HAS BEEN ***VERY*** NAUGHTY, MISTER 8.
HOW WAS I MEANT TO KNOW IT WAS AN EVIL PLANT?!
YOU KNOW NOTHING, NUMBER 8.
WELL, AT LEAST WE'RE ALL FINE. SO IT'S A HAPPY ENDING, RIGHT?!
ERR, SURE.
SFFMMM
I HAVE GOT TO ELIMINATE THAT RIDICULOUSLY CUTE MINION.
EYE OF THE PLANT
EVIL PLAN: FAIL
THIS ISN'T THE END, EVIL PENGUIN. I WILL PREVAIL NEXT TIME!!!

THE STINKING TRUTH

GAH! I'VE BEEN RACKING MY BRAINS FOR A MONTH AND *STILL* CAN'T THINK OF A WORTHY DOMINATION PLAN!

PLINK

OH, AND NOW I'VE DROPPED MY FAVORITE PEN!

EUGENE, GO PICK THAT UP FOR ME...

DOMINATE THE PLANET

I WILL RULE!

NO PLAN

ME

HUMA

YES, EV-

PARP!

OH!

THAT WAS COMPLETELY UNEXPECTED, EVIL MASTER.

EUREKA! THAT'S IT!!!

YOUR REAR END HAS INSPIRED ME, EUGENE. WELL DONE!

ERM, THANK YOU?

THE NEXT DAY

LET ME PRESENT TO YOU MY LATEST WORLD DOMINATION PLAN...

THE *FEROCIOUS AND REALLY TERRIBLE* MACHINE!

STENCH

STENCH

SIR... I'M NOT SURE IF YOU'RE AWARE, BUT THE INITIALS SPELL OUT-

SHH SHH... NO MORE SPEAKING, NUMBER 8. NO MORE...

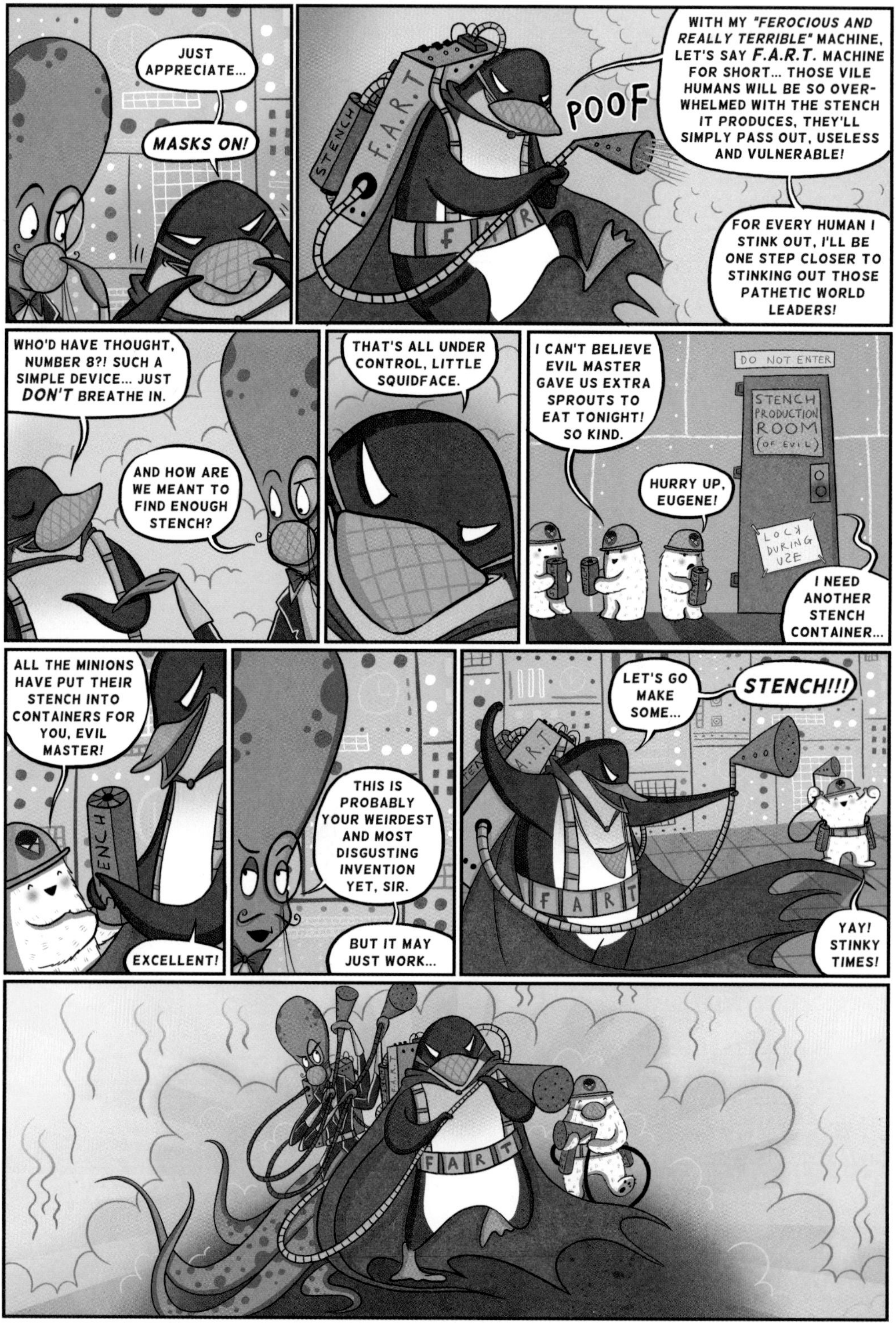

JUST APPRECIATE...
MASKS ON!
POOF
WITH MY "FEROCIOUS AND REALLY TERRIBLE" MACHINE, LET'S SAY F.A.R.T. MACHINE FOR SHORT... THOSE VILE HUMANS WILL BE SO OVERWHELMED WITH THE STENCH IT PRODUCES, THEY'LL SIMPLY PASS OUT, USELESS AND VULNERABLE!
FOR EVERY HUMAN I STINK OUT, I'LL BE ONE STEP CLOSER TO STINKING OUT THOSE PATHETIC WORLD LEADERS!
STENCH
F.A.R.T
F A R T
WHO'D HAVE THOUGHT, NUMBER 8?! SUCH A SIMPLE DEVICE... JUST DON'T BREATHE IN.
AND HOW ARE WE MEANT TO FIND ENOUGH STENCH?
THAT'S ALL UNDER CONTROL, LITTLE SQUIDFACE.
I CAN'T BELIEVE EVIL MASTER GAVE US EXTRA SPROUTS TO EAT TONIGHT! SO KIND.
DO NOT ENTER
STENCH PRODUCTION ROOM (OF EVIL)
HURRY UP, EUGENE!
LOCK DURING USE
I NEED ANOTHER STENCH CONTAINER...
ALL THE MINIONS HAVE PUT THEIR STENCH INTO CONTAINERS FOR YOU, EVIL MASTER!
EXCELLENT!
THIS IS PROBABLY YOUR WEIRDEST AND MOST DISGUSTING INVENTION YET, SIR.
BUT IT MAY JUST WORK...
LET'S GO MAKE SOME...
STENCH!!!
YAY! STINKY TIMES!
F A R T

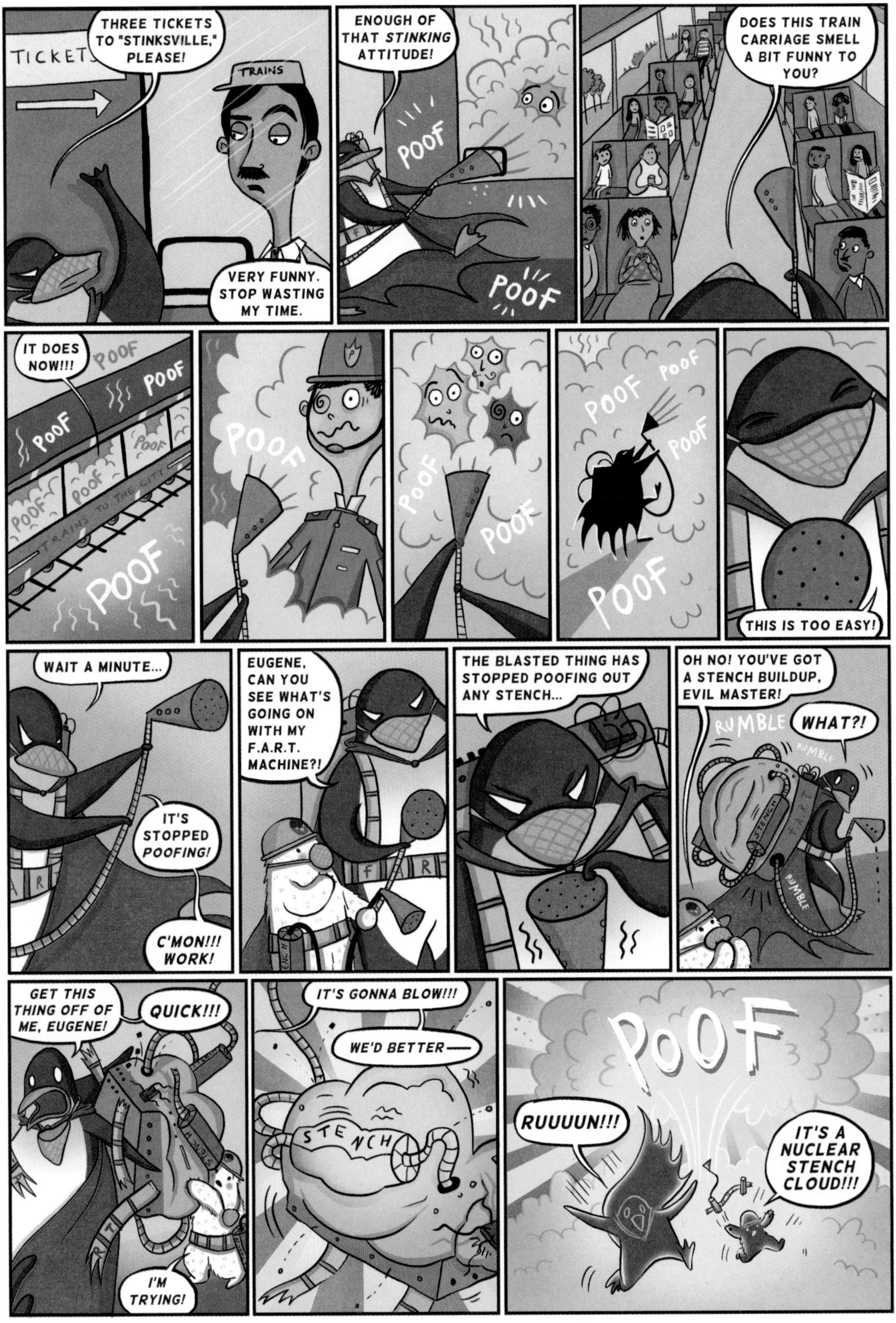
TICKETS
THREE TICKETS TO "STINKSVILLE," PLEASE!
TRAINS
VERY FUNNY. STOP WASTING MY TIME.
ENOUGH OF THAT *STINKING* ATTITUDE!
POOF
POOF
DOES THIS TRAIN CARRIAGE SMELL A BIT FUNNY TO YOU?
IT DOES NOW!!!
POOF
POOF
POOF
POOF
POOF
POOF
TRAINS TO THE CITY
POOF
POOF
POOF
POOF
POOF
POOF
POOF
POOF
POOF
THIS IS TOO EASY!
WAIT A MINUTE...
IT'S STOPPED POOFING!
C'MON!!! WORK!
EUGENE, CAN YOU SEE WHAT'S GOING ON WITH MY F.A.R.T. MACHINE?!
THE BLASTED THING HAS STOPPED POOFING OUT ANY STENCH...
OH NO! YOU'VE GOT A STENCH BUILDUP, EVIL MASTER!
RUMBLE
WHAT?!
RUMBLE
RUMBLE
GET THIS THING OFF OF ME, EUGENE!
QUICK!!!
I'M TRYING!
IT'S GONNA BLOW!!!
WE'D BETTER—
STENCH
POOF
RUUUUN!!!
IT'S A NUCLEAR STENCH CLOUD!!!

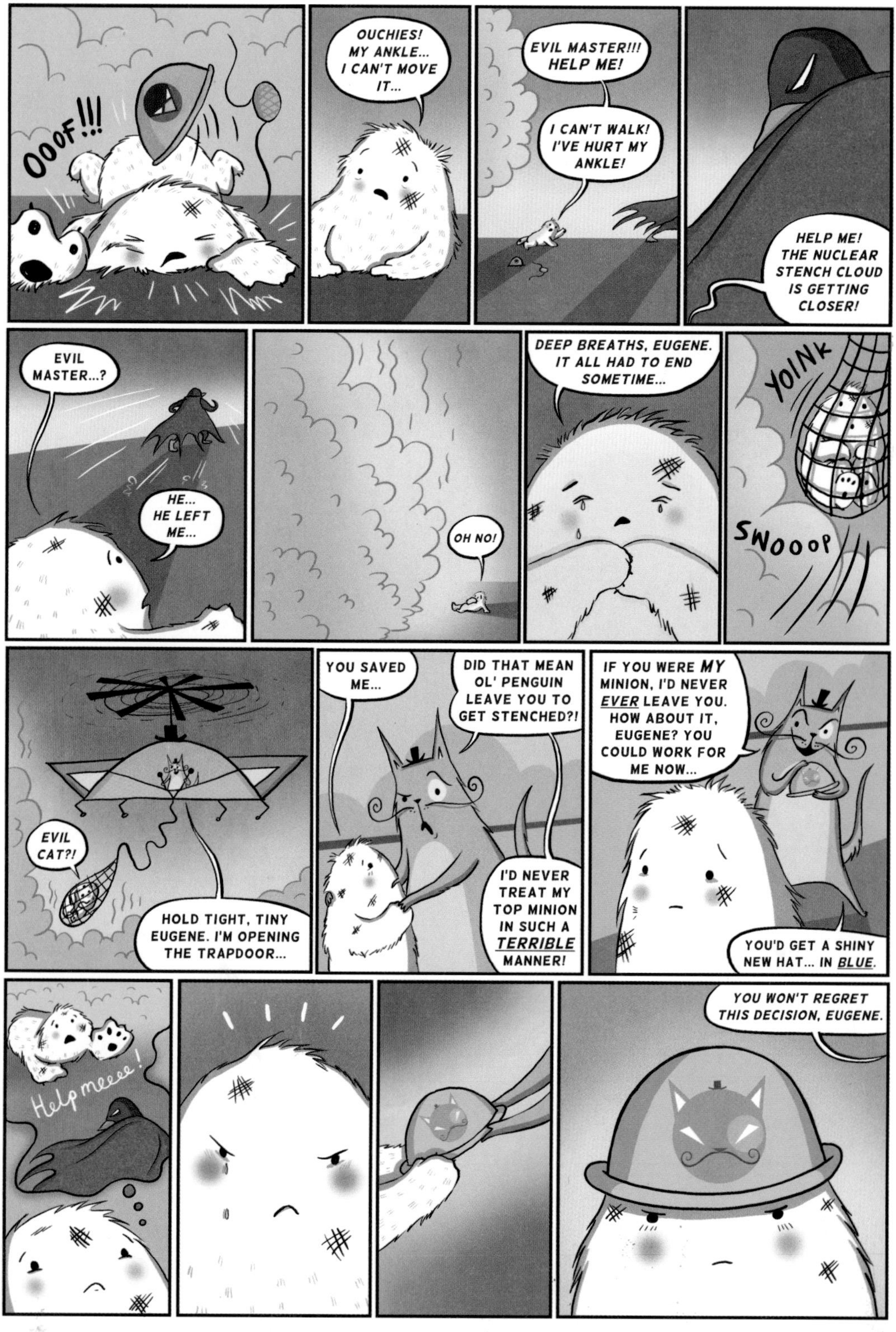
OOOF!!!
OUCHIES! MY ANKLE... I CAN'T MOVE IT...
EVIL MASTER!!! HELP ME!
I CAN'T WALK! I'VE HURT MY ANKLE!
HELP ME! THE NUCLEAR STENCH CLOUD IS GETTING CLOSER!
EVIL MASTER...?
HE... HE LEFT ME...
OH NO!
DEEP BREATHS, EUGENE. IT ALL HAD TO END SOMETIME...
YOINK
SWOOOP
EVIL CAT?!
HOLD TIGHT, TINY EUGENE. I'M OPENING THE TRAPDOOR...
YOU SAVED ME...
DID THAT MEAN OL' PENGUIN LEAVE YOU TO GET STENCHED?!
I'D NEVER TREAT MY TOP MINION IN SUCH A TERRIBLE MANNER!
IF YOU WERE MY MINION, I'D NEVER EVER LEAVE YOU. HOW ABOUT IT, EUGENE? YOU COULD WORK FOR ME NOW...
YOU'D GET A SHINY NEW HAT... IN BLUE.
Help meeee!
YOU WON'T REGRET THIS DECISION, EUGENE.

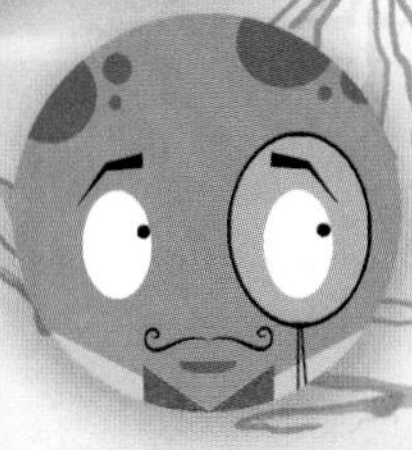

Please Exit for the Domination Station: Part 1

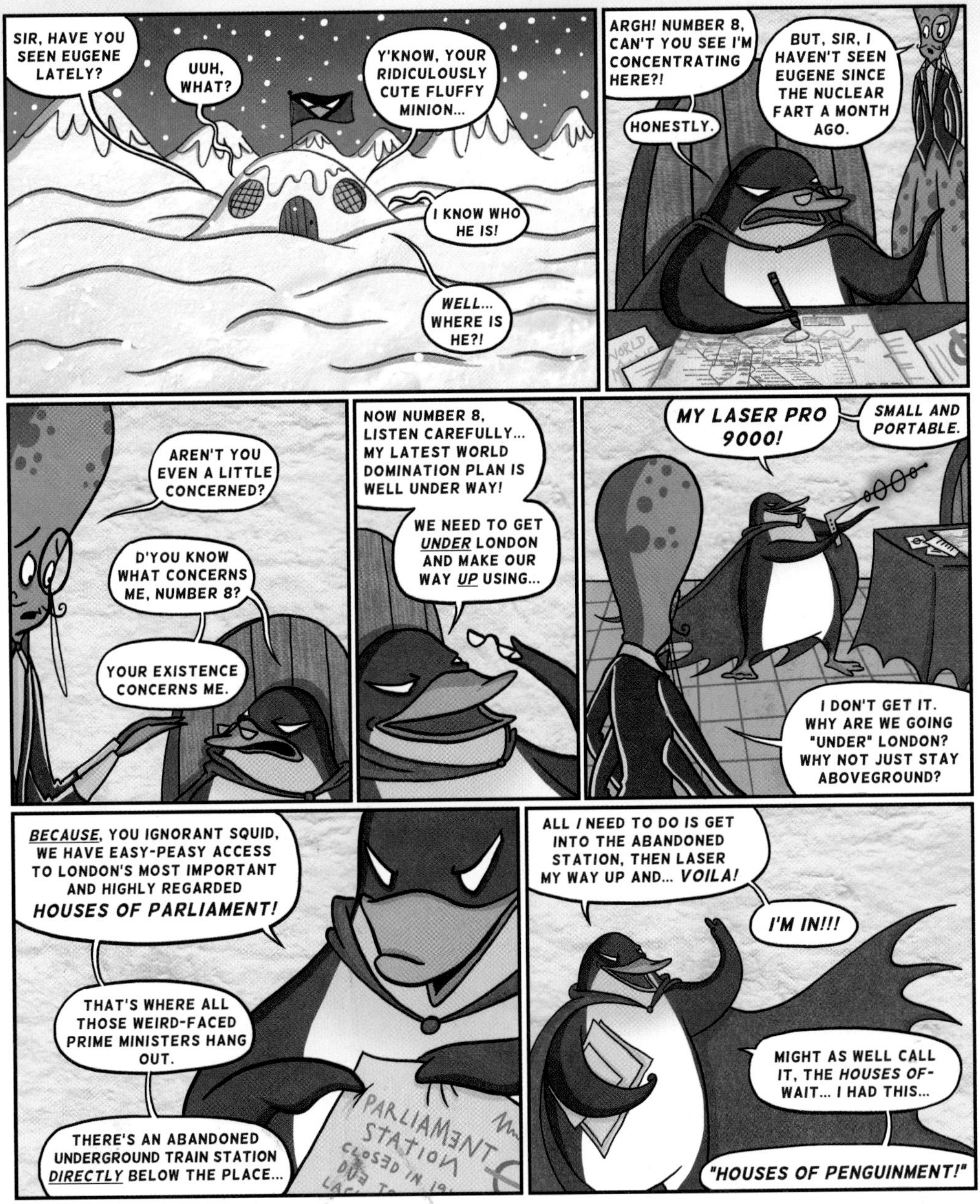

SIR, HAVE YOU SEEN EUGENE LATELY?
UUH, WHAT?
Y'KNOW, YOUR RIDICULOUSLY CUTE FLUFFY MINION...
I KNOW WHO HE IS!
WELL... WHERE IS HE?!
ARGH! NUMBER 8, CAN'T YOU SEE I'M CONCENTRATING HERE?!
HONESTLY.
BUT, SIR, I HAVEN'T SEEN EUGENE SINCE THE NUCLEAR FART A MONTH AGO.
AREN'T YOU EVEN A LITTLE CONCERNED?
D'YOU KNOW WHAT CONCERNS ME, NUMBER 8?
YOUR EXISTENCE CONCERNS ME.
NOW NUMBER 8, LISTEN CAREFULLY... MY LATEST WORLD DOMINATION PLAN IS WELL UNDER WAY!
WE NEED TO GET *UNDER* LONDON AND MAKE OUR WAY *UP* USING...
MY LASER PRO 9000!
SMALL AND PORTABLE.
I DON'T GET IT. WHY ARE WE GOING "UNDER" LONDON? WHY NOT JUST STAY ABOVEGROUND?
BECAUSE, YOU IGNORANT SQUID, WE HAVE EASY-PEASY ACCESS TO LONDON'S MOST IMPORTANT AND HIGHLY REGARDED *HOUSES OF PARLIAMENT!*
THAT'S WHERE ALL THOSE WEIRD-FACED PRIME MINISTERS HANG OUT.
THERE'S AN ABANDONED UNDERGROUND TRAIN STATION *DIRECTLY* BELOW THE PLACE...
PARLIAMENT STATION
ALL *I* NEED TO DO IS GET INTO THE ABANDONED STATION, THEN LASER MY WAY UP AND... *VOILA!*
I'M IN!!!
MIGHT AS WELL CALL IT, THE *HOUSES OF-* WAIT... I HAD THIS...
"HOUSES OF PENGUINMENT!"

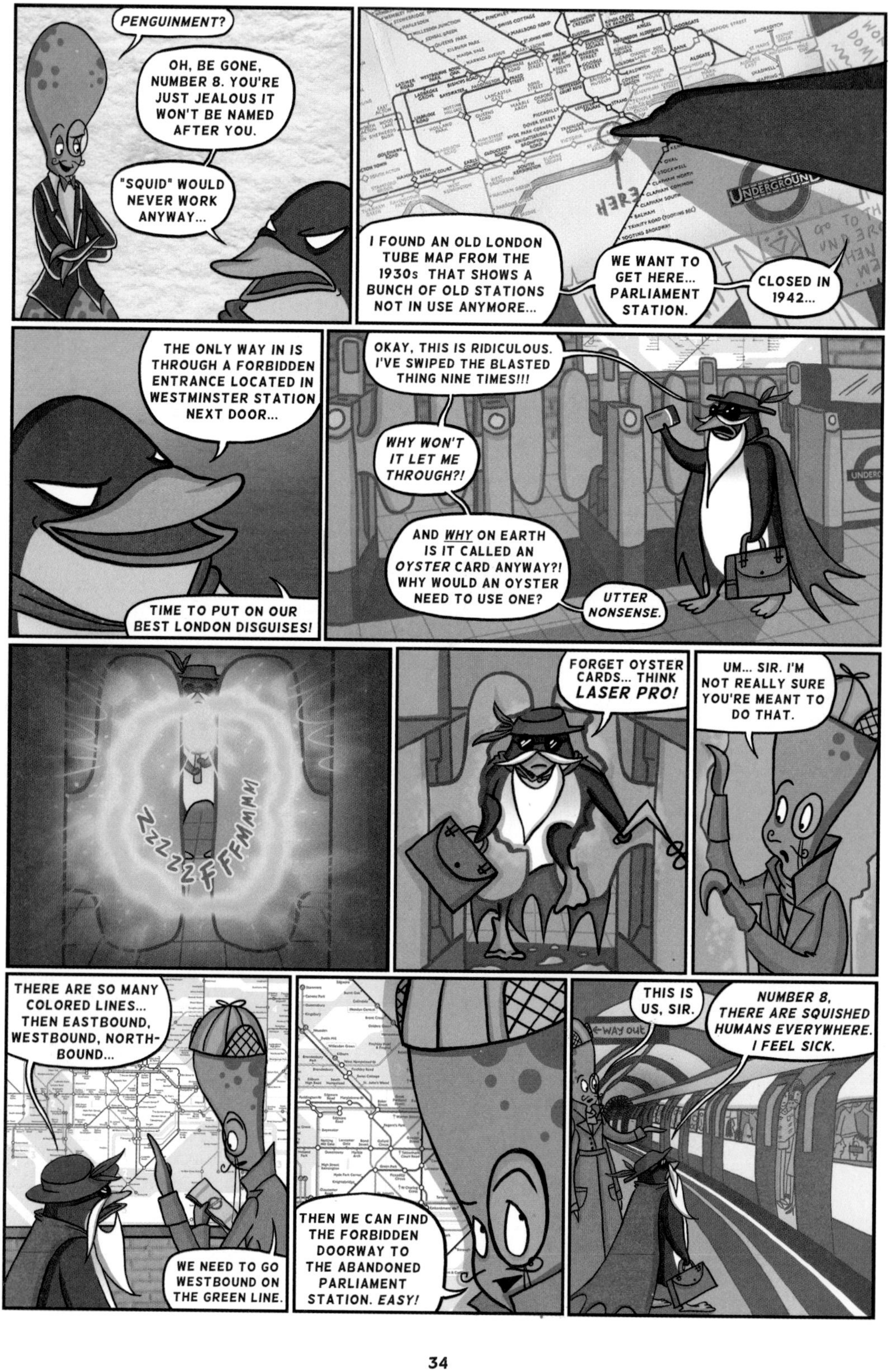
PENGUINMENT?
OH, BE GONE, NUMBER 8. YOU'RE JUST JEALOUS IT WON'T BE NAMED AFTER YOU.
"SQUID" WOULD NEVER WORK ANYWAY...
HERE
UNDERGROUND
I FOUND AN OLD LONDON TUBE MAP FROM THE 1930s THAT SHOWS A BUNCH OF OLD STATIONS NOT IN USE ANYMORE...
WE WANT TO GET HERE... PARLIAMENT STATION.
CLOSED IN 1942...
THE ONLY WAY IN IS THROUGH A FORBIDDEN ENTRANCE LOCATED IN WESTMINSTER STATION NEXT DOOR...
TIME TO PUT ON OUR BEST LONDON DISGUISES!
OKAY, THIS IS RIDICULOUS. I'VE SWIPED THE BLASTED THING NINE TIMES!!!
WHY WON'T IT LET ME THROUGH?!
AND WHY ON EARTH IS IT CALLED AN OYSTER CARD ANYWAY?! WHY WOULD AN OYSTER NEED TO USE ONE?
UTTER NONSENSE.
ZZZZZFFFMMMM
FORGET OYSTER CARDS... THINK LASER PRO!
UM... SIR. I'M NOT REALLY SURE YOU'RE MEANT TO DO THAT.
THERE ARE SO MANY COLORED LINES... THEN EASTBOUND, WESTBOUND, NORTH-BOUND...
WE NEED TO GO WESTBOUND ON THE GREEN LINE.
THEN WE CAN FIND THE FORBIDDEN DOORWAY TO THE ABANDONED PARLIAMENT STATION. EASY!
WAY OUT
THIS IS US, SIR.
NUMBER 8, THERE ARE SQUISHED HUMANS EVERYWHERE. I FEEL SICK.

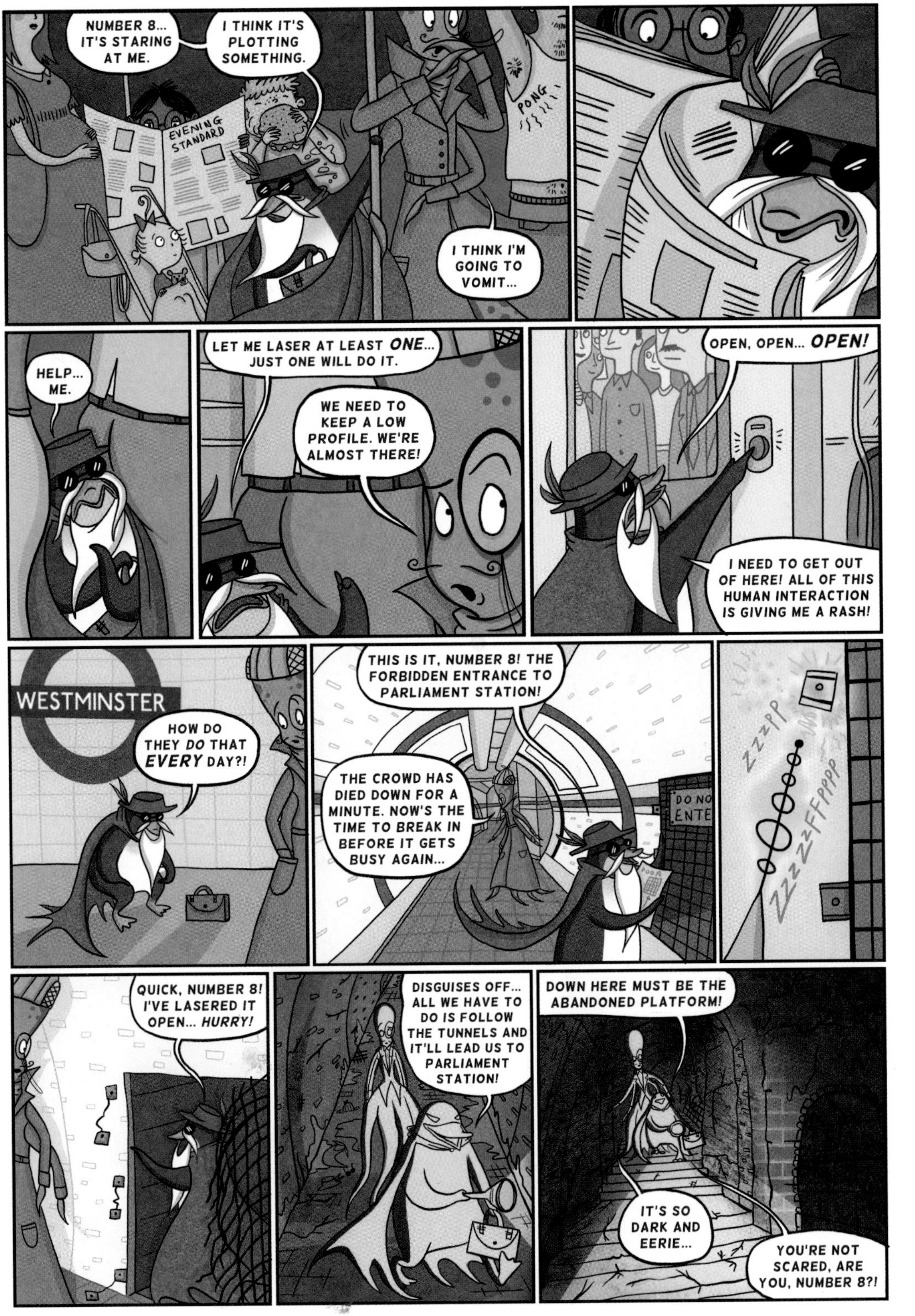
NUMBER 8... IT'S STARING AT ME.
I THINK IT'S PLOTTING SOMETHING.
EVENING STANDARD
PONG
I THINK I'M GOING TO VOMIT...
HELP... ME.
LET ME LASER AT LEAST ONE... JUST ONE WILL DO IT.
WE NEED TO KEEP A LOW PROFILE. WE'RE ALMOST THERE!
OPEN, OPEN... OPEN!
I NEED TO GET OUT OF HERE! ALL OF THIS HUMAN INTERACTION IS GIVING ME A RASH!
WESTMINSTER
HOW DO THEY DO THAT EVERY DAY?!
THIS IS IT, NUMBER 8! THE FORBIDDEN ENTRANCE TO PARLIAMENT STATION!
THE CROWD HAS DIED DOWN FOR A MINUTE. NOW'S THE TIME TO BREAK IN BEFORE IT GETS BUSY AGAIN...
DO NO
ENTE
ZZZPP
ZZZZFFPPPP
QUICK, NUMBER 8! I'VE LASERED IT OPEN... HURRY!
DISGUISES OFF... ALL WE HAVE TO DO IS FOLLOW THE TUNNELS AND IT'LL LEAD US TO PARLIAMENT STATION!
DOWN HERE MUST BE THE ABANDONED PLATFORM!
IT'S SO DARK AND EERIE...
YOU'RE NOT SCARED, ARE YOU, NUMBER 8?!

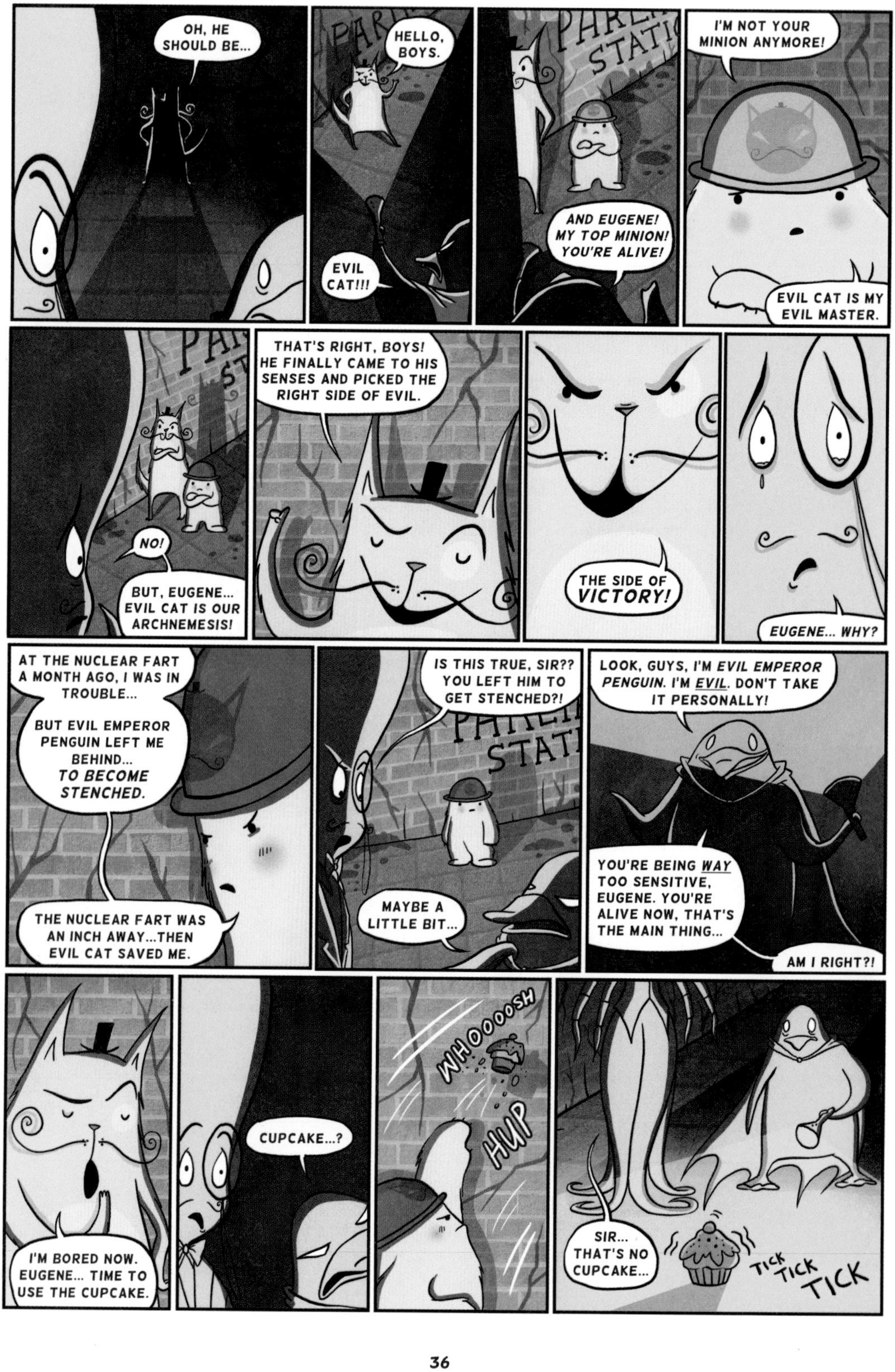
OH, HE SHOULD BE...
PAR
HELLO, BOYS.
EVIL CAT!!!
PAREN STATI
AND EUGENE! MY TOP MINION! YOU'RE ALIVE!
I'M NOT YOUR MINION ANYMORE!
EVIL CAT IS MY EVIL MASTER.
NO!
BUT, EUGENE... EVIL CAT IS OUR ARCHNEMESIS!
THAT'S RIGHT, BOYS! HE FINALLY CAME TO HIS SENSES AND PICKED THE RIGHT SIDE OF EVIL.
THE SIDE OF VICTORY!
EUGENE... WHY?
AT THE NUCLEAR FART A MONTH AGO, I WAS IN TROUBLE...
BUT EVIL EMPEROR PENGUIN LEFT ME BEHIND... TO BECOME STENCHED.
THE NUCLEAR FART WAS AN INCH AWAY...THEN EVIL CAT SAVED ME.
IS THIS TRUE, SIR?? YOU LEFT HIM TO GET STENCHED?!
MAYBE A LITTLE BIT...
LOOK, GUYS, I'M EVIL EMPEROR PENGUIN. I'M EVIL. DON'T TAKE IT PERSONALLY!
YOU'RE BEING WAY TOO SENSITIVE, EUGENE. YOU'RE ALIVE NOW, THAT'S THE MAIN THING...
AM I RIGHT?!
I'M BORED NOW. EUGENE... TIME TO USE THE CUPCAKE.
CUPCAKE...?
WHOOOOSH
HUP
SIR... THAT'S NO CUPCAKE...
TICK TICK TICK

Please Exit for the Domination Station: Part 2

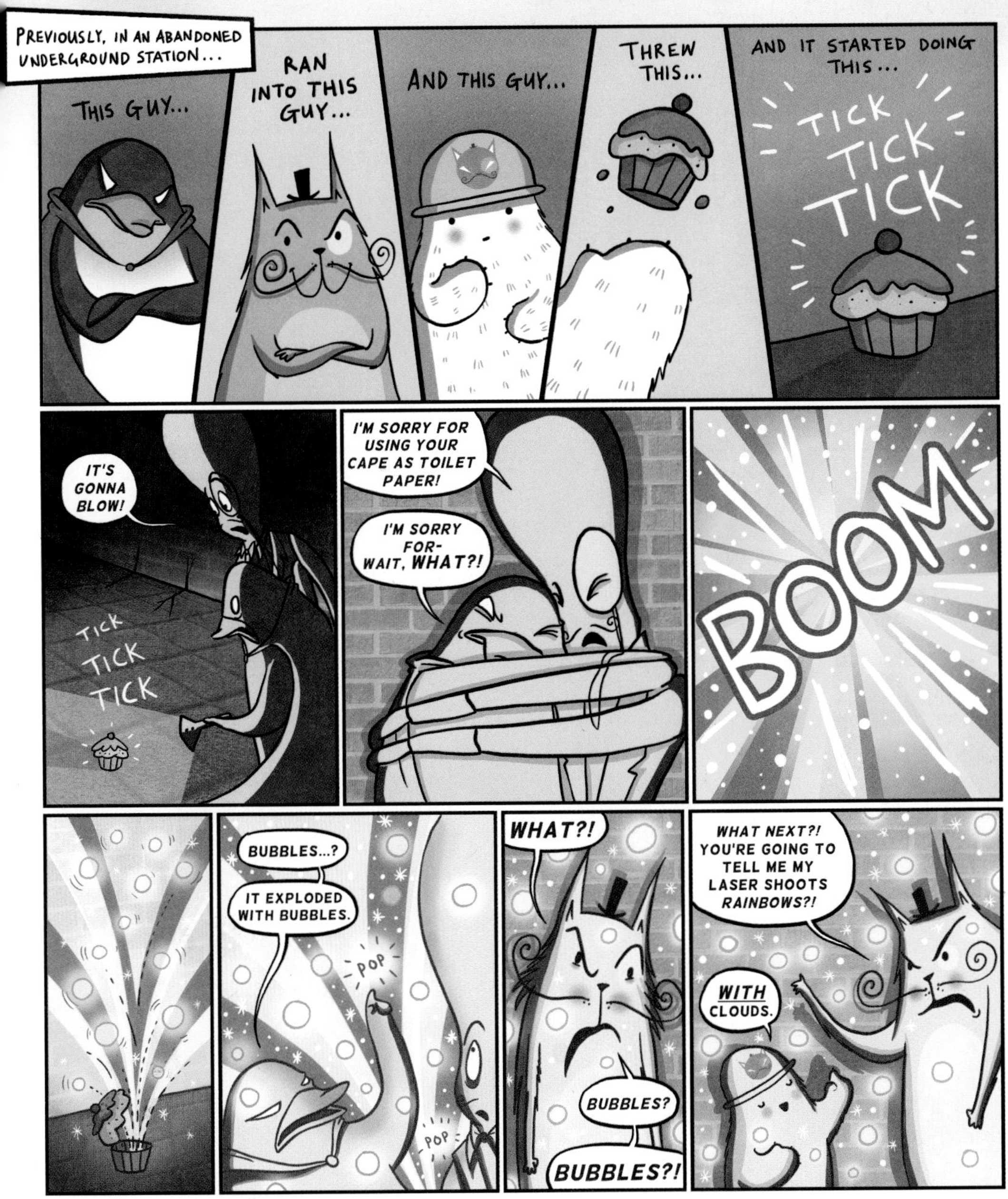
PREVIOUSLY, IN AN ABANDONED UNDERGROUND STATION...
THIS GUY...
RAN INTO THIS GUY...
AND THIS GUY...
THREW THIS...
AND IT STARTED DOING THIS...
TICK TICK TICK
IT'S GONNA BLOW!
TICK TICK TICK
I'M SORRY FOR USING YOUR CAPE AS TOILET PAPER!
I'M SORRY FOR- WAIT, WHAT?!
BOOM
BUBBLES...?
IT EXPLODED WITH BUBBLES.
POP
POP
WHAT?!
BUBBLES?
BUBBLES?!
WHAT NEXT?! YOU'RE GOING TO TELL ME MY LASER SHOOTS RAINBOWS?!
WITH CLOUDS.

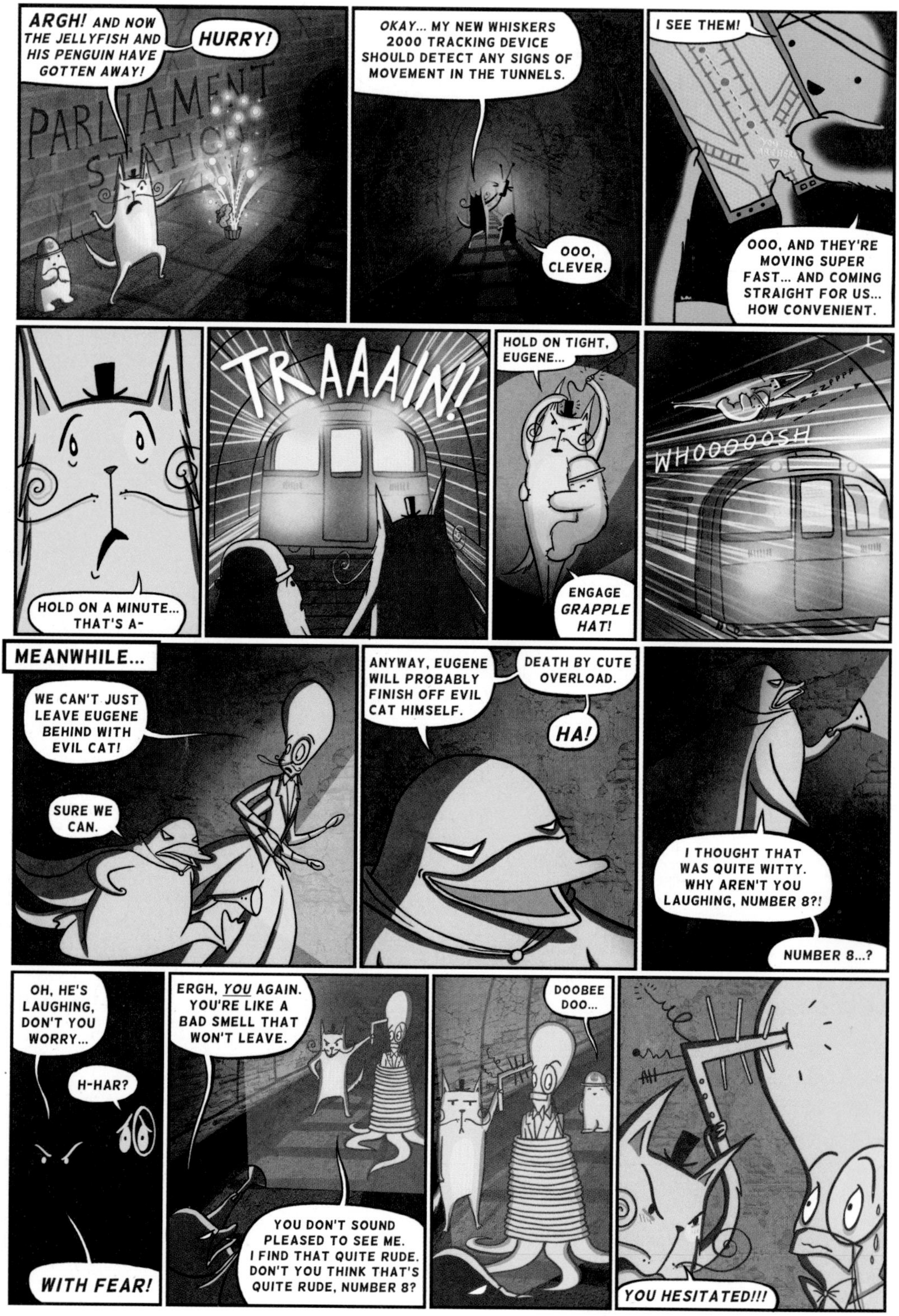
ARGH! AND NOW THE JELLYFISH AND HIS PENGUIN HAVE GOTTEN AWAY!
HURRY!
PARLIAMENT STATION
OKAY... MY NEW WHISKERS 2000 TRACKING DEVICE SHOULD DETECT ANY SIGNS OF MOVEMENT IN THE TUNNELS.
OOO, CLEVER.
I SEE THEM!
OOO, AND THEY'RE MOVING SUPER FAST... AND COMING STRAIGHT FOR US... HOW CONVENIENT.
HOLD ON A MINUTE... THAT'S A-
TRAAAIN!
HOLD ON TIGHT, EUGENE...
ENGAGE GRAPPLE HAT!
WHOOOOOOSH
MEANWHILE...
WE CAN'T JUST LEAVE EUGENE BEHIND WITH EVIL CAT!
SURE WE CAN.
ANYWAY, EUGENE WILL PROBABLY FINISH OFF EVIL CAT HIMSELF.
DEATH BY CUTE OVERLOAD.
HA!
I THOUGHT THAT WAS QUITE WITTY. WHY AREN'T YOU LAUGHING, NUMBER 8?!
NUMBER 8...?
OH, HE'S LAUGHING, DON'T YOU WORRY...
H-HAR?
WITH FEAR!
ERGH, YOU AGAIN. YOU'RE LIKE A BAD SMELL THAT WON'T LEAVE.
YOU DON'T SOUND PLEASED TO SEE ME. I FIND THAT QUITE RUDE. DON'T YOU THINK THAT'S QUITE RUDE, NUMBER 8?
DOOBEE DOO...
YOU HESITATED!!!

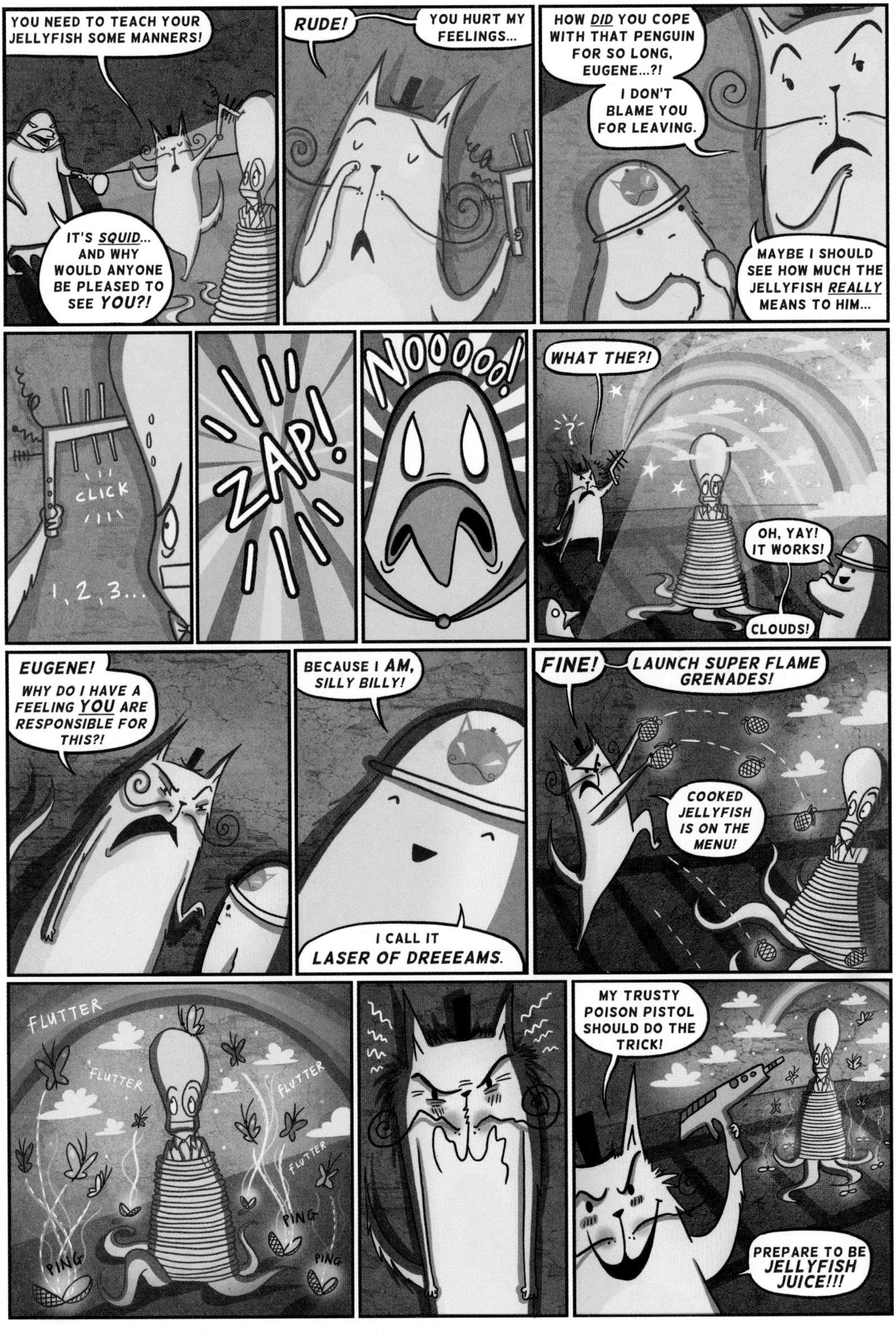
YOU NEED TO TEACH YOUR JELLYFISH SOME MANNERS!
IT'S SQUID... AND WHY WOULD ANYONE BE PLEASED TO SEE YOU?!
RUDE!
YOU HURT MY FEELINGS...
HOW DID YOU COPE WITH THAT PENGUIN FOR SO LONG, EUGENE...?!
I DON'T BLAME YOU FOR LEAVING.
MAYBE I SHOULD SEE HOW MUCH THE JELLYFISH REALLY MEANS TO HIM...
CLICK
1, 2, 3...
ZAP!
NOOOOO!
WHAT THE?!
OH, YAY! IT WORKS!
CLOUDS!
EUGENE!
WHY DO I HAVE A FEELING YOU ARE RESPONSIBLE FOR THIS?!
BECAUSE I AM, SILLY BILLY!
I CALL IT LASER OF DREEEAMS.
FINE!
LAUNCH SUPER FLAME GRENADES!
COOKED JELLYFISH IS ON THE MENU!
FLUTTER
FLUTTER
FLUTTER
FLUTTER
PING
PING
PING
MY TRUSTY POISON PISTOL SHOULD DO THE TRICK!
PREPARE TO BE JELLYFISH JUICE!!!

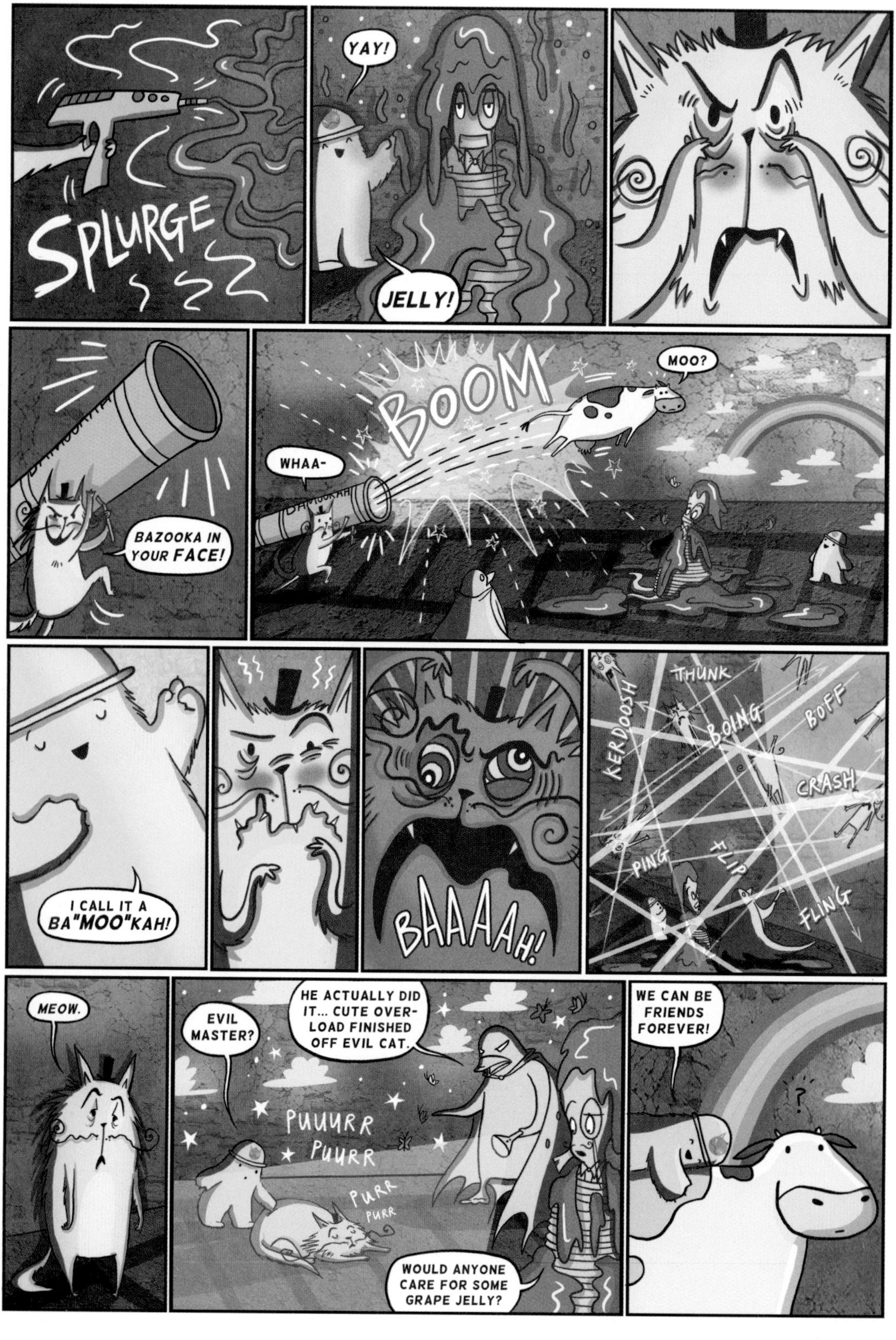
SPLURGE
YAY!
JELLY!
BAZOOKA IN YOUR FACE!
WHAA-
BOOM
MOO?
I CALL IT A BA"MOO"KAH!
BAAAAAH!
THUNK
KERDOOSH
BOING
BOFF
CRASH
PING
FLIP
FLING
MEOW.
EVIL MASTER?
HE ACTUALLY DID IT... CUTE OVER-LOAD FINISHED OFF EVIL CAT.
PUUURR
PUURR
PURR
PURR
WOULD ANYONE CARE FOR SOME GRAPE JELLY?
WE CAN BE FRIENDS FOREVER!
?

HEAD IN THE CLOUDS

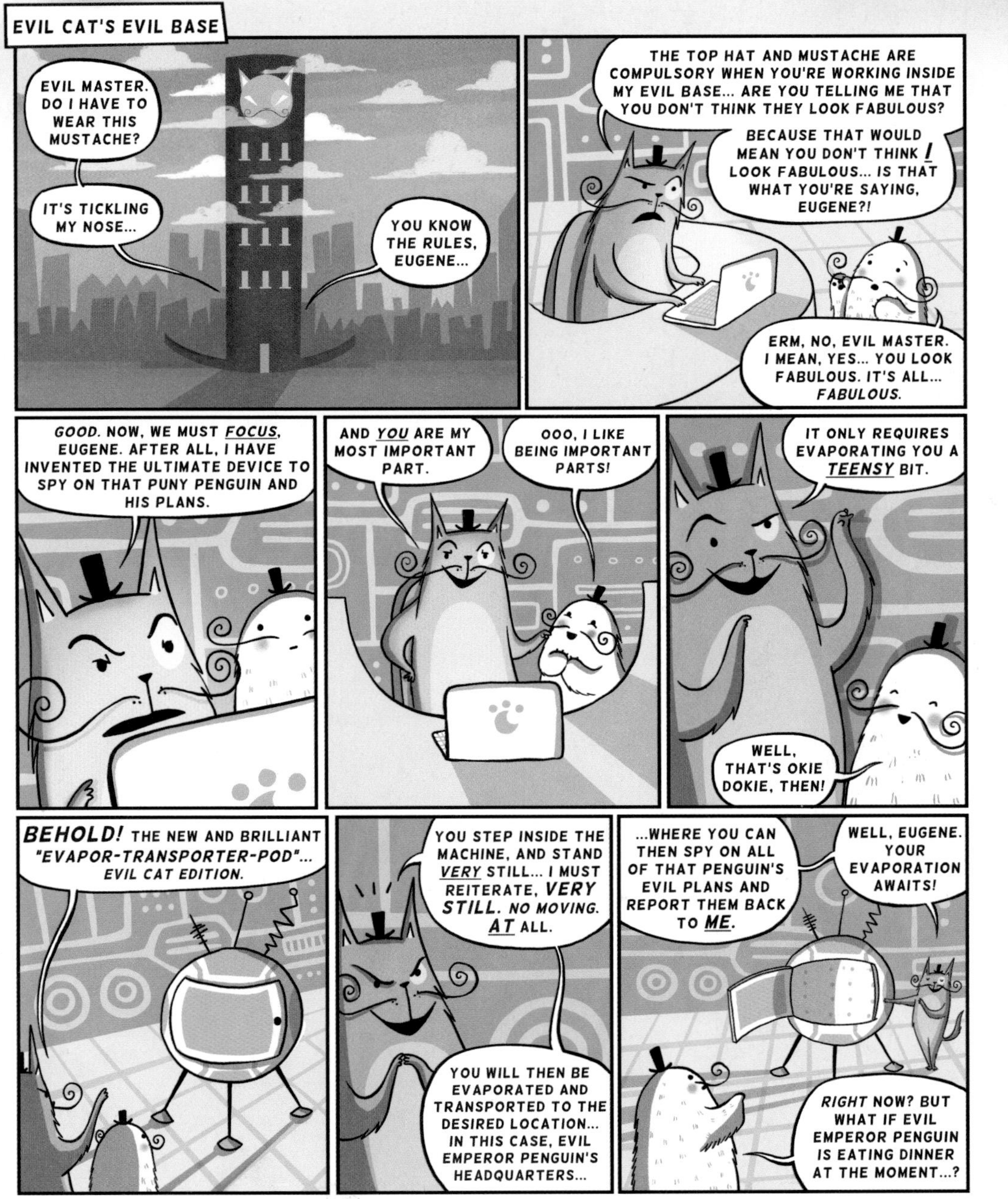

EVIL CAT'S EVIL BASE
EVIL MASTER. DO I HAVE TO WEAR THIS MUSTACHE?
IT'S TICKLING MY NOSE...
YOU KNOW THE RULES, EUGENE...
THE TOP HAT AND MUSTACHE ARE COMPULSORY WHEN YOU'RE WORKING INSIDE MY EVIL BASE... ARE YOU TELLING ME THAT YOU DON'T THINK THEY LOOK FABULOUS?
BECAUSE THAT WOULD MEAN YOU DON'T THINK I LOOK FABULOUS... IS THAT WHAT YOU'RE SAYING, EUGENE?!
ERM, NO, EVIL MASTER. I MEAN, YES... YOU LOOK FABULOUS. IT'S ALL... FABULOUS.
GOOD. NOW, WE MUST FOCUS, EUGENE. AFTER ALL, I HAVE INVENTED THE ULTIMATE DEVICE TO SPY ON THAT PUNY PENGUIN AND HIS PLANS.
AND YOU ARE MY MOST IMPORTANT PART.
OOO, I LIKE BEING IMPORTANT PARTS!
IT ONLY REQUIRES EVAPORATING YOU A TEENSY BIT.
WELL, THAT'S OKIE DOKIE, THEN!
BEHOLD! THE NEW AND BRILLIANT "EVAPOR-TRANSPORTER-POD"... EVIL CAT EDITION.
YOU STEP INSIDE THE MACHINE, AND STAND VERY STILL... I MUST REITERATE, VERY STILL. NO MOVING. AT ALL.
YOU WILL THEN BE EVAPORATED AND TRANSPORTED TO THE DESIRED LOCATION... IN THIS CASE, EVIL EMPEROR PENGUIN'S HEADQUARTERS...
...WHERE YOU CAN THEN SPY ON ALL OF THAT PENGUIN'S EVIL PLANS AND REPORT THEM BACK TO ME.
WELL, EUGENE. YOUR EVAPORATION AWAITS!
RIGHT NOW? BUT WHAT IF EVIL EMPEROR PENGUIN IS EATING DINNER AT THE MOMENT...?

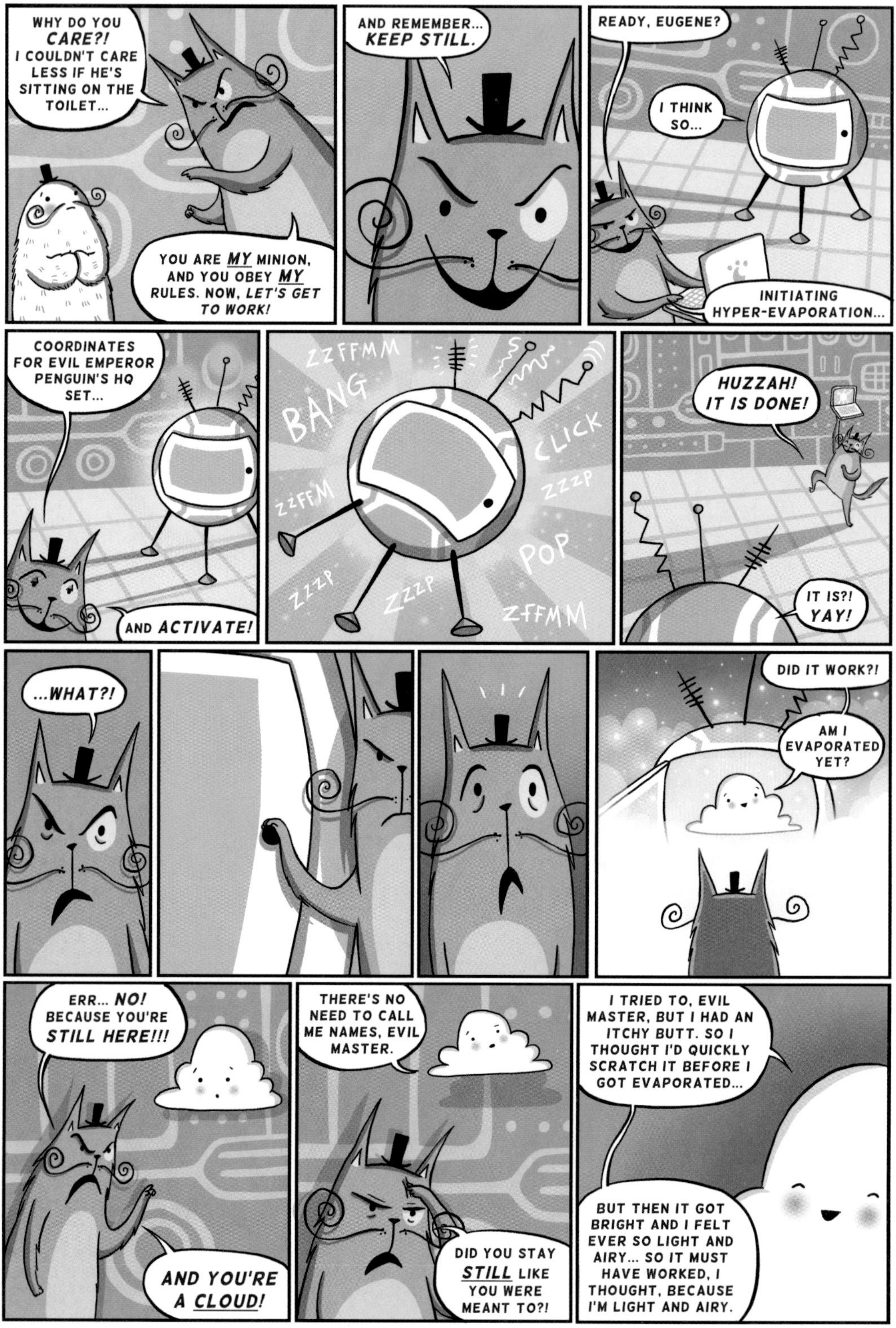
WHY DO YOU CARE?! I COULDN'T CARE LESS IF HE'S SITTING ON THE TOILET...
YOU ARE MY MINION, AND YOU OBEY MY RULES. NOW, LET'S GET TO WORK!
AND REMEMBER... KEEP STILL.
READY, EUGENE?
I THINK SO...
INITIATING HYPER-EVAPORATION...
COORDINATES FOR EVIL EMPEROR PENGUIN'S HQ SET...
AND ACTIVATE!
ZZFFMM
BANG
CLICK
ZZZP
ZZFFM
POP
ZZZP
ZZZP
ZFFMM
HUZZAH! IT IS DONE!
IT IS?! YAY!
...WHAT?!
DID IT WORK?!
AM I EVAPORATED YET?
ERR... NO! BECAUSE YOU'RE STILL HERE!!!
AND YOU'RE A CLOUD!
THERE'S NO NEED TO CALL ME NAMES, EVIL MASTER.
DID YOU STAY STILL LIKE YOU WERE MEANT TO?!
I TRIED TO, EVIL MASTER, BUT I HAD AN ITCHY BUTT. SO I THOUGHT I'D QUICKLY SCRATCH IT BEFORE I GOT EVAPORATED...
BUT THEN IT GOT BRIGHT AND I FELT EVER SO LIGHT AND AIRY... SO IT MUST HAVE WORKED, I THOUGHT, BECAUSE I'M LIGHT AND AIRY.

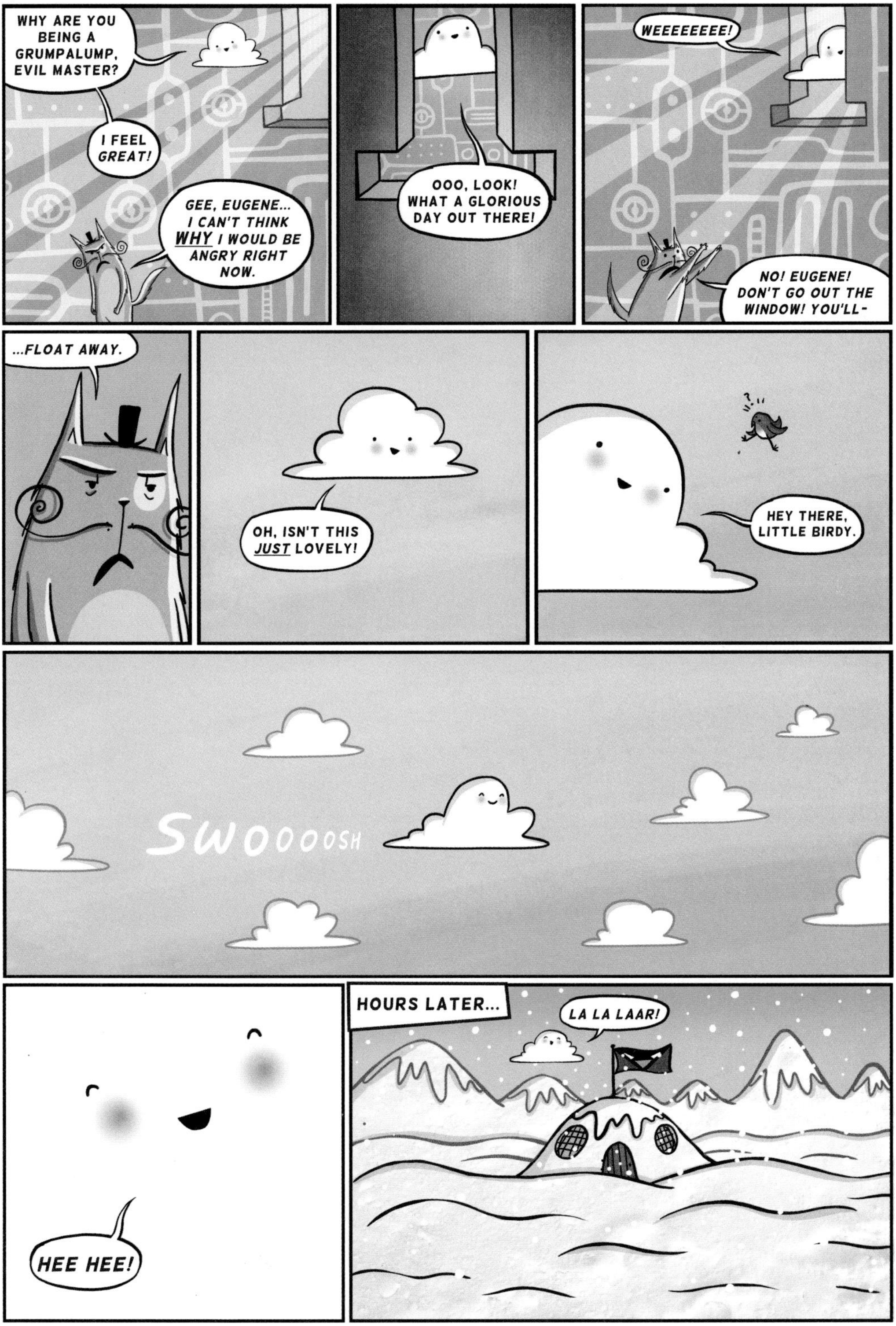
WHY ARE YOU BEING A GRUMPALUMP, EVIL MASTER?
I FEEL GREAT!
GEE, EUGENE... I CAN'T THINK WHY I WOULD BE ANGRY RIGHT NOW.
OOO, LOOK! WHAT A GLORIOUS DAY OUT THERE!
WEEEEEEEE!
NO! EUGENE! DON'T GO OUT THE WINDOW! YOU'LL-
...FLOAT AWAY.
OH, ISN'T THIS JUST LOVELY!
HEY THERE, LITTLE BIRDY.
SWOOOOOSH
HEE HEE!
HOURS LATER...
LA LA LAAR!

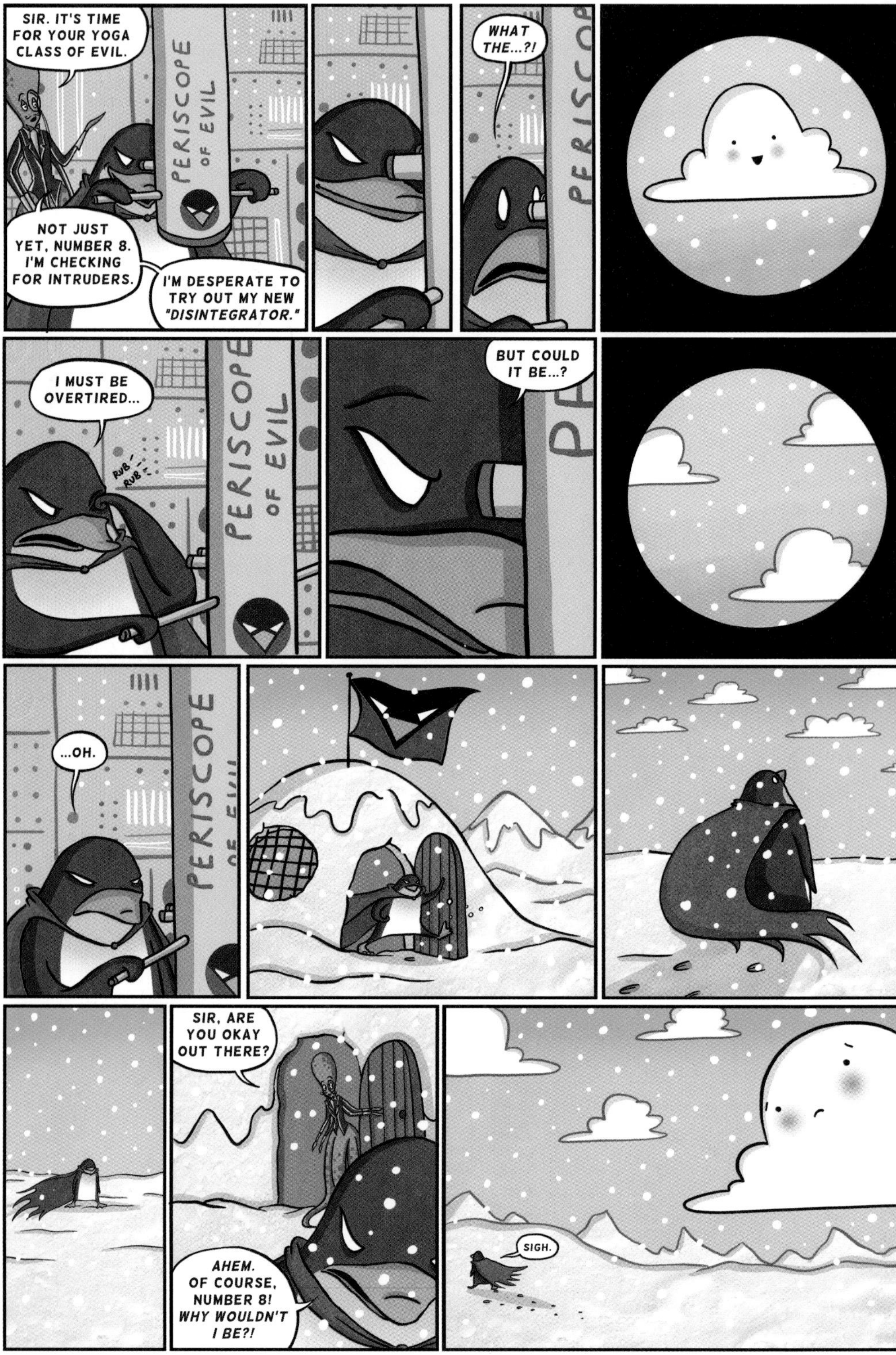
SIR. IT'S TIME FOR YOUR YOGA CLASS OF EVIL.
PERISCOPE OF EVIL
NOT JUST YET, NUMBER 8. I'M CHECKING FOR INTRUDERS.
I'M DESPERATE TO TRY OUT MY NEW "DISINTEGRATOR."
WHAT THE...?!
I MUST BE OVERTIRED...
RUB RUB
BUT COULD IT BE...?
...OH.
SIR, ARE YOU OKAY OUT THERE?
AHEM. OF COURSE, NUMBER 8! WHY WOULDN'T I BE?!
SIGH.

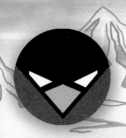

Sibling Rivalry: Part 1

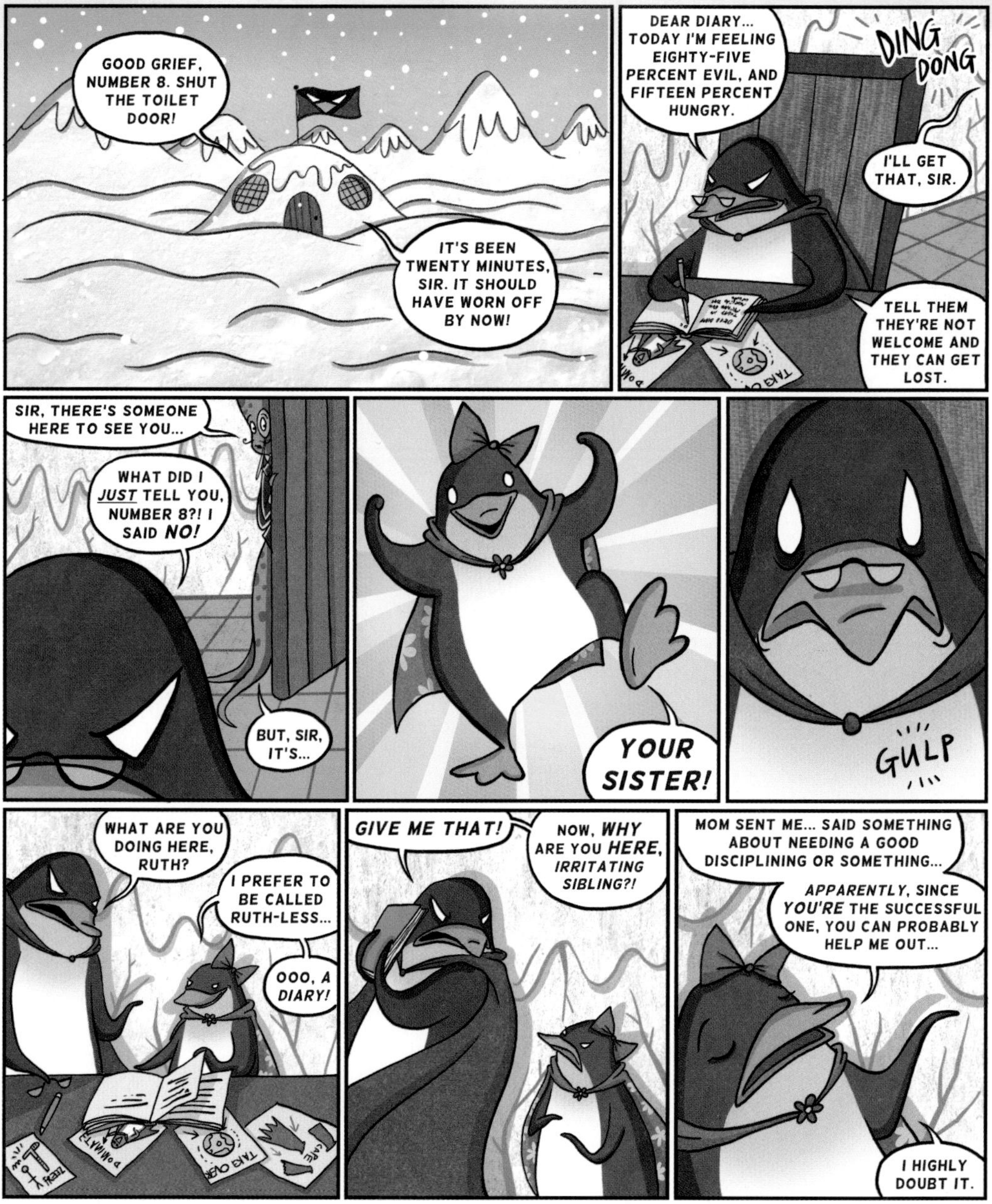

GOOD GRIEF, NUMBER 8. SHUT THE TOILET DOOR!
IT'S BEEN TWENTY MINUTES, SIR. IT SHOULD HAVE WORN OFF BY NOW!
DEAR DIARY... TODAY I'M FEELING EIGHTY-FIVE PERCENT EVIL, AND FIFTEEN PERCENT HUNGRY.
DING DONG
I'LL GET THAT, SIR.
TELL THEM THEY'RE NOT WELCOME AND THEY CAN GET LOST.
SIR, THERE'S SOMEONE HERE TO SEE YOU...
WHAT DID I JUST TELL YOU, NUMBER 8?! I SAID NO!
BUT, SIR, IT'S...
YOUR SISTER!
GULP
WHAT ARE YOU DOING HERE, RUTH?
I PREFER TO BE CALLED RUTH-LESS...
OOO, A DIARY!
GIVE ME THAT!
NOW, WHY ARE YOU HERE, IRRITATING SIBLING?!
MOM SENT ME... SAID SOMETHING ABOUT NEEDING A GOOD DISCIPLINING OR SOMETHING...
APPARENTLY, SINCE YOU'RE THE SUCCESSFUL ONE, YOU CAN PROBABLY HELP ME OUT...
I HIGHLY DOUBT IT.

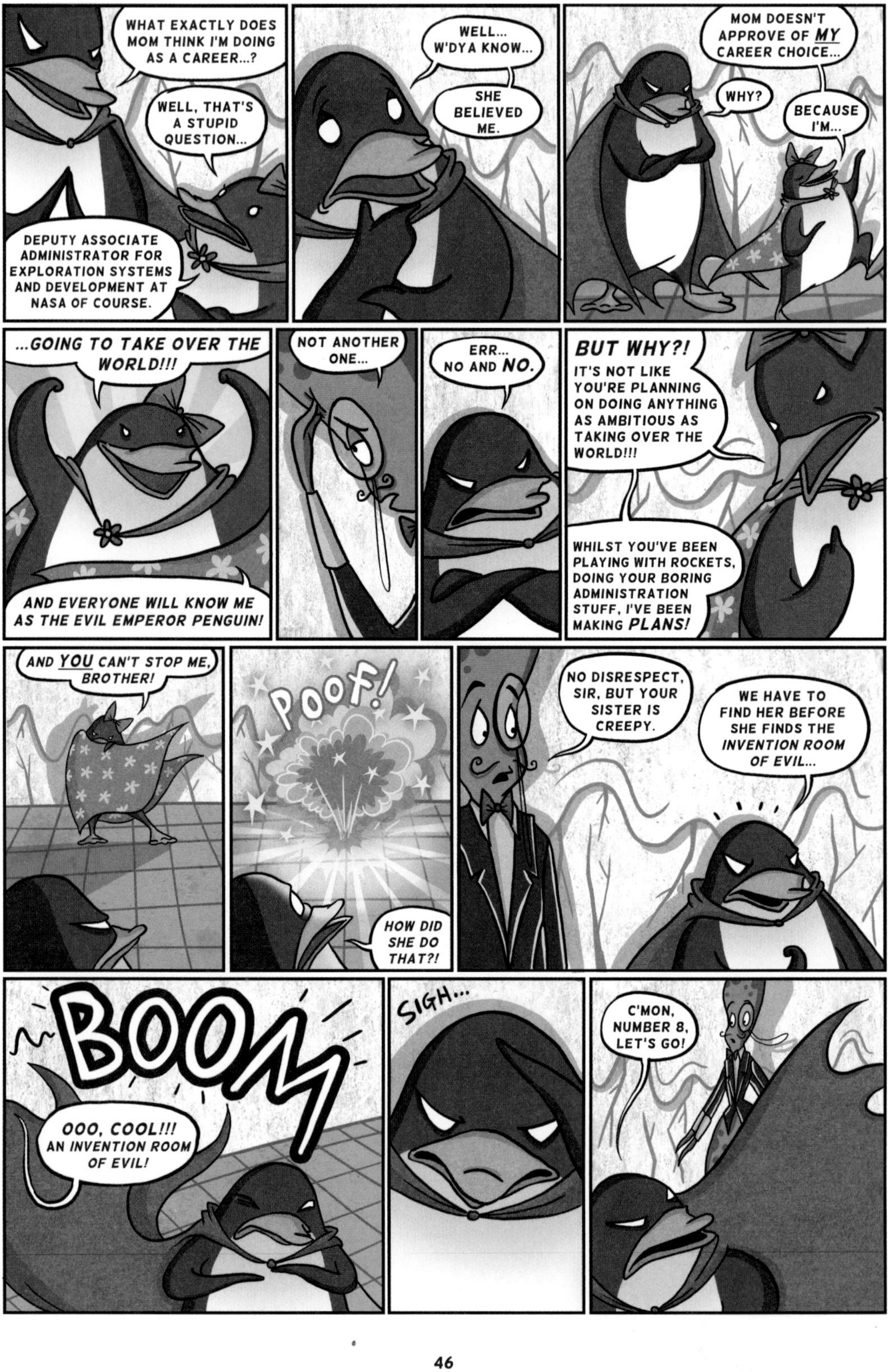
WHAT EXACTLY DOES MOM THINK I'M DOING AS A CAREER...?
WELL, THAT'S A STUPID QUESTION...
DEPUTY ASSOCIATE ADMINISTRATOR FOR EXPLORATION SYSTEMS AND DEVELOPMENT AT NASA OF COURSE.
WELL... W'DYA KNOW...
SHE BELIEVED ME.
MOM DOESN'T APPROVE OF MY CAREER CHOICE...
WHY?
BECAUSE I'M...
...GOING TO TAKE OVER THE WORLD!!!
AND EVERYONE WILL KNOW ME AS THE EVIL EMPEROR PENGUIN!
NOT ANOTHER ONE...
ERR... NO AND NO.
BUT WHY?! IT'S NOT LIKE YOU'RE PLANNING ON DOING ANYTHING AS AMBITIOUS AS TAKING OVER THE WORLD!!!
WHILST YOU'VE BEEN PLAYING WITH ROCKETS, DOING YOUR BORING ADMINISTRATION STUFF, I'VE BEEN MAKING PLANS!
AND YOU CAN'T STOP ME, BROTHER!
POOF!
HOW DID SHE DO THAT?!
NO DISRESPECT, SIR, BUT YOUR SISTER IS CREEPY.
WE HAVE TO FIND HER BEFORE SHE FINDS THE INVENTION ROOM OF EVIL...
BOOM
OOO, COOL!!! AN INVENTION ROOM OF EVIL!
SIGH...
C'MON, NUMBER 8, LET'S GO!

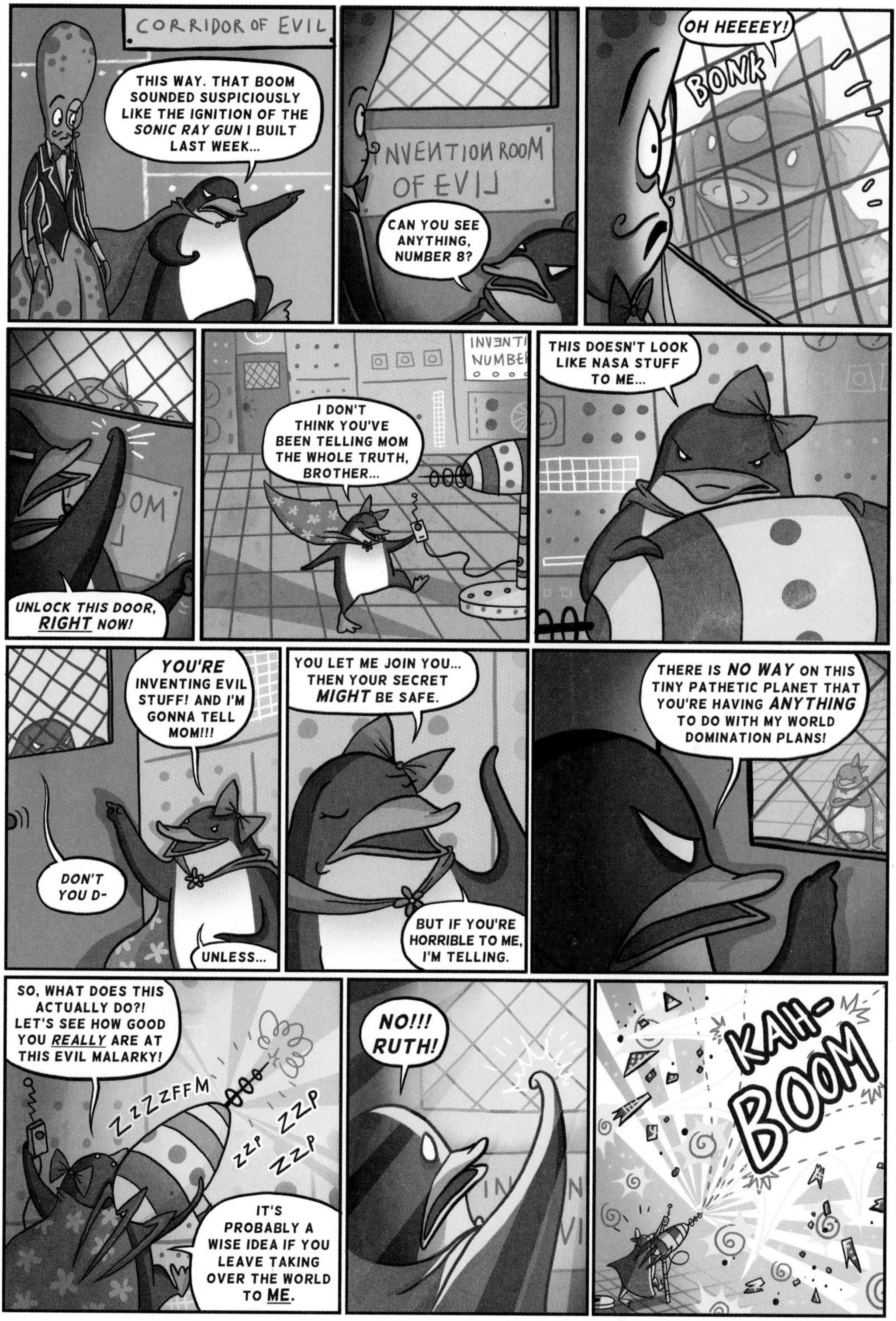

CORRIDOR OF EVIL
THIS WAY. THAT BOOM SOUNDED SUSPICIOUSLY LIKE THE IGNITION OF THE *SONIC RAY GUN* I BUILT LAST WEEK...
INVENTION ROOM OF EVIL
CAN YOU SEE ANYTHING, NUMBER 8?
OH HEEEEY!
BONK
UNLOCK THIS DOOR, RIGHT NOW!
I DON'T THINK YOU'VE BEEN TELLING MOM THE WHOLE TRUTH, BROTHER...
THIS DOESN'T LOOK LIKE NASA STUFF TO ME...
YOU'RE INVENTING EVIL STUFF! AND I'M GONNA TELL MOM!!!
DON'T YOU D-
UNLESS...
YOU LET ME JOIN YOU... THEN YOUR SECRET *MIGHT* BE SAFE.
BUT IF YOU'RE HORRIBLE TO ME, I'M TELLING.
THERE IS *NO WAY* ON THIS TINY PATHETIC PLANET THAT YOU'RE HAVING *ANYTHING* TO DO WITH MY WORLD DOMINATION PLANS!
SO, WHAT DOES THIS ACTUALLY DO?! LET'S SEE HOW GOOD YOU *REALLY* ARE AT THIS EVIL MALARKY!
ZZZZFFM
ZZP ZZP ZZP
IT'S PROBABLY A WISE IDEA IF YOU LEAVE TAKING OVER THE WORLD TO ME.
NO!!! RUTH!
KAH-BOOM

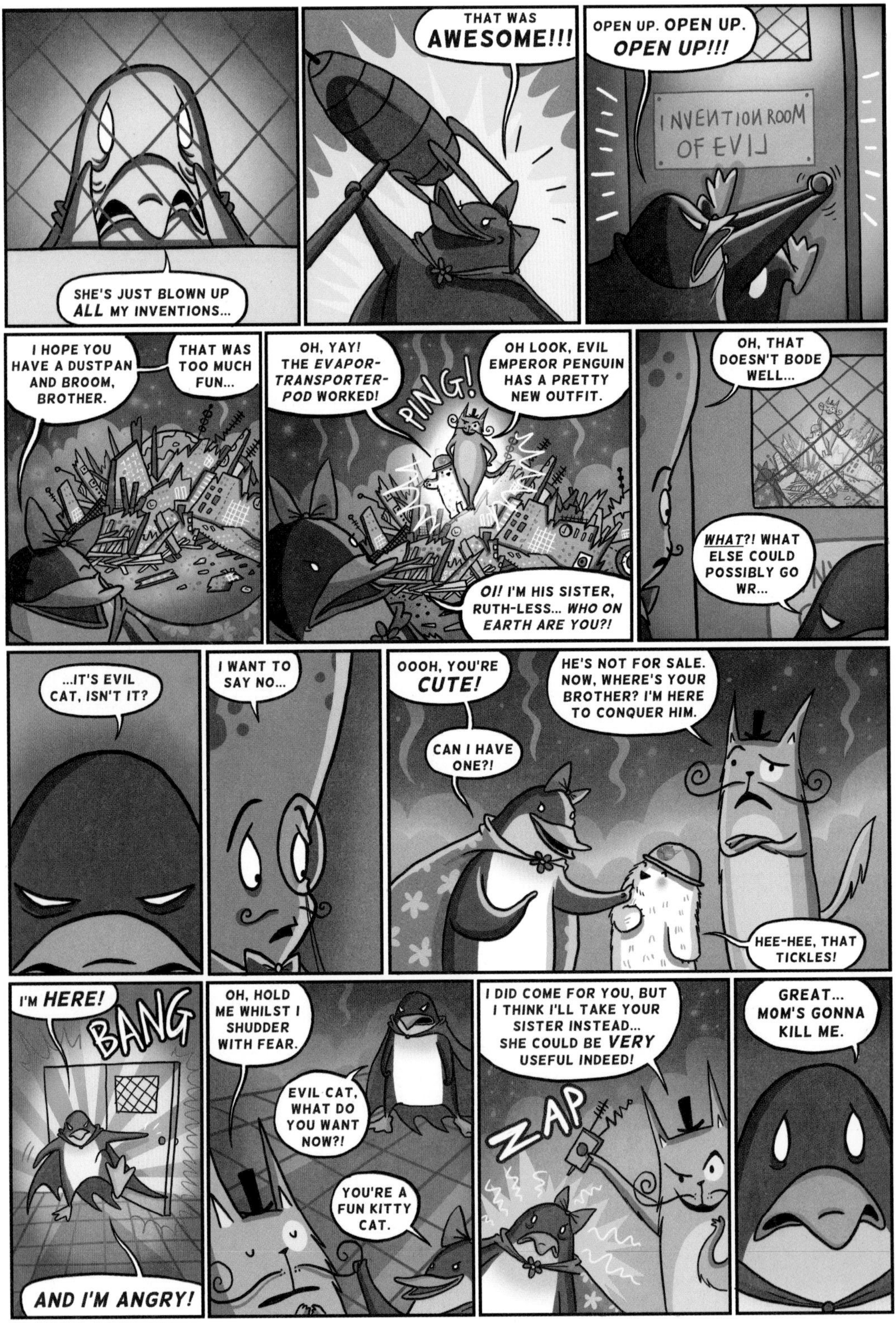
SHE'S JUST BLOWN UP *ALL* MY INVENTIONS...
THAT WAS AWESOME!!!
OPEN UP. OPEN UP. *OPEN UP!!!*
INVENTION ROOM OF EVIL
I HOPE YOU HAVE A DUSTPAN AND BROOM, BROTHER.
THAT WAS TOO MUCH FUN...
OH, YAY! THE *EVAPOR-TRANSPORTER-POD* WORKED!
PING!
OH LOOK, EVIL EMPEROR PENGUIN HAS A PRETTY NEW OUTFIT.
OI! I'M HIS SISTER, RUTH-LESS... *WHO ON EARTH ARE YOU?!*
OH, THAT DOESN'T BODE WELL...
WHAT?! WHAT ELSE COULD POSSIBLY GO WR...
...IT'S EVIL CAT, ISN'T IT?
I WANT TO SAY NO...
OOOH, YOU'RE *CUTE!*
CAN I HAVE ONE?!
HE'S NOT FOR SALE. NOW, WHERE'S YOUR BROTHER? I'M HERE TO CONQUER HIM.
HEE-HEE, THAT TICKLES!
I'M *HERE!*
BANG
AND I'M ANGRY!
OH, HOLD ME WHILST I SHUDDER WITH FEAR.
EVIL CAT, WHAT DO YOU WANT NOW?!
YOU'RE A FUN KITTY CAT.
I DID COME FOR YOU, BUT I THINK I'LL TAKE YOUR SISTER INSTEAD... SHE COULD BE *VERY* USEFUL INDEED!
ZAP
GREAT... MOM'S GONNA KILL ME.

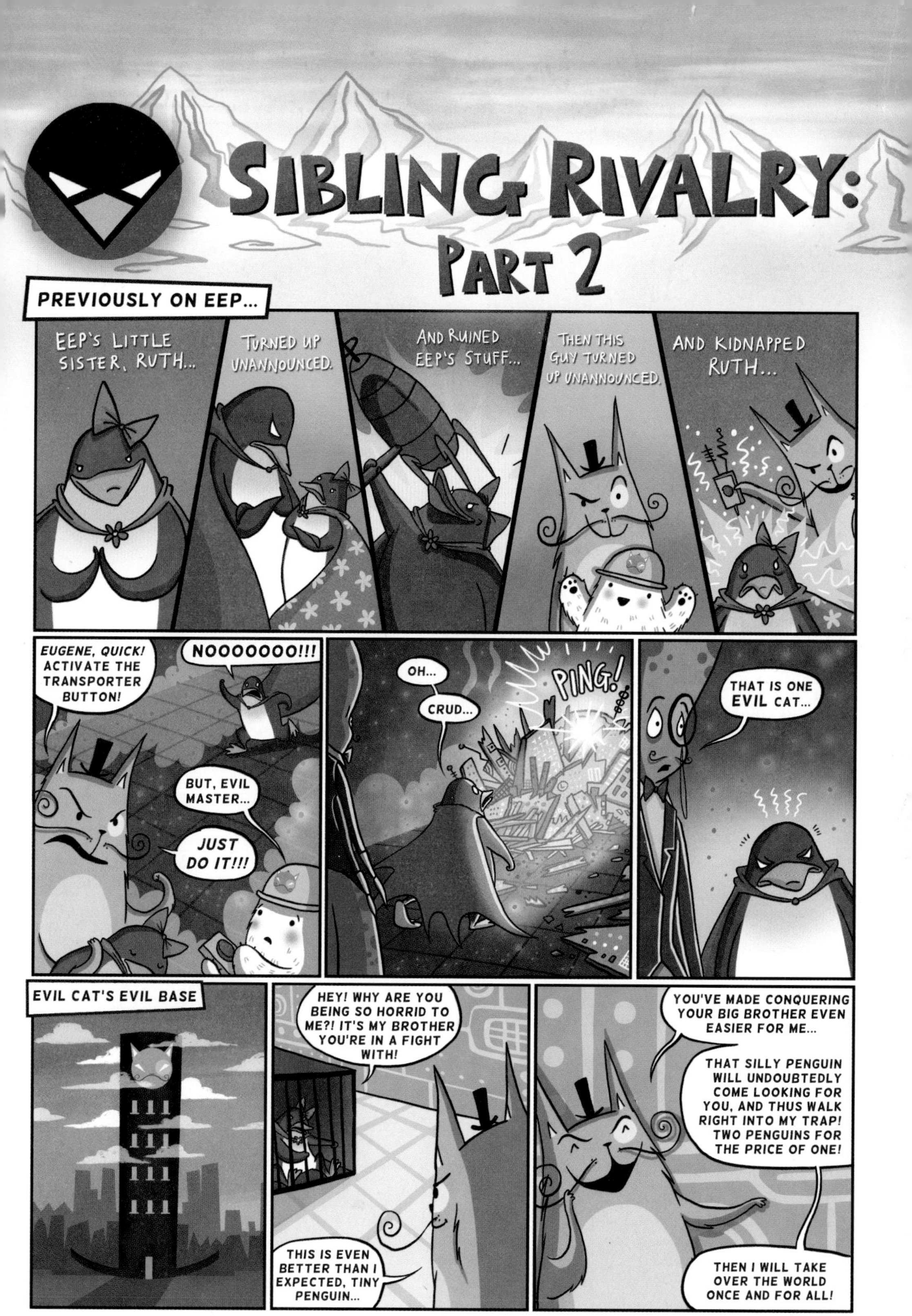
SIBLING RIVALRY: PART 2
PREVIOUSLY ON EEP...
EEP'S LITTLE SISTER, RUTH...
TURNED UP UNANNOUNCED.
AND RUINED EEP'S STUFF...
THEN THIS GUY TURNED UP UNANNOUNCED.
AND KIDNAPPED RUTH...
EUGENE, QUICK! ACTIVATE THE TRANSPORTER BUTTON!
NOOOOOOO!!!
BUT, EVIL MASTER...
JUST DO IT!!!
OH...
CRUD...
PING!
THAT IS ONE EVIL CAT...
EVIL CAT'S EVIL BASE
HEY! WHY ARE YOU BEING SO HORRID TO ME?! IT'S MY BROTHER YOU'RE IN A FIGHT WITH!
THIS IS EVEN BETTER THAN I EXPECTED, TINY PENGUIN...
YOU'VE MADE CONQUERING YOUR BIG BROTHER EVEN EASIER FOR ME...
THAT SILLY PENGUIN WILL UNDOUBTEDLY COME LOOKING FOR YOU, AND THUS WALK RIGHT INTO MY TRAP! TWO PENGUINS FOR THE PRICE OF ONE!
THEN I WILL TAKE OVER THE WORLD ONCE AND FOR ALL!

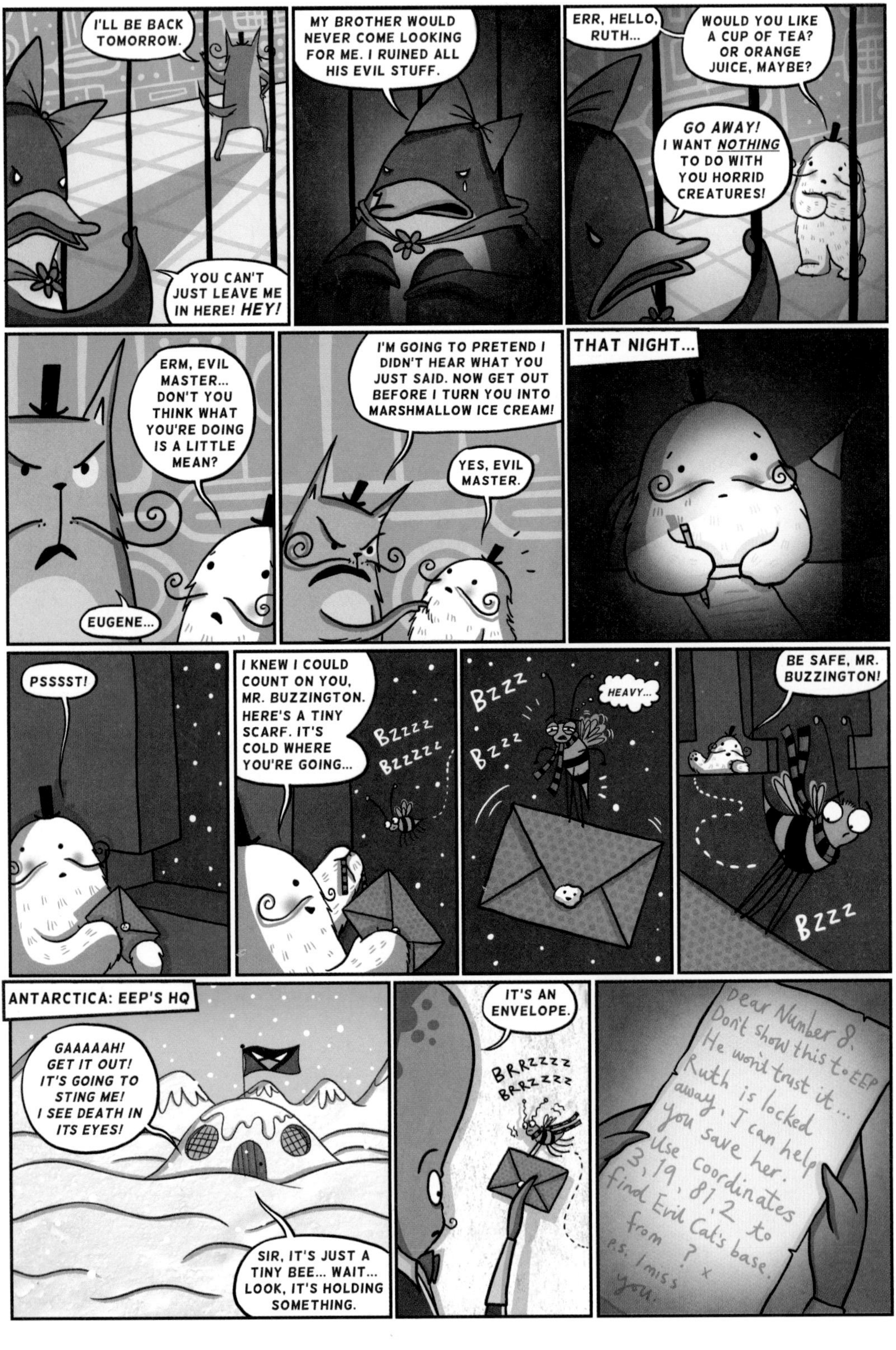
I'LL BE BACK TOMORROW.
YOU CAN'T JUST LEAVE ME IN HERE! HEY!
MY BROTHER WOULD NEVER COME LOOKING FOR ME. I RUINED ALL HIS EVIL STUFF.
ERR, HELLO, RUTH...
WOULD YOU LIKE A CUP OF TEA? OR ORANGE JUICE, MAYBE?
GO AWAY! I WANT NOTHING TO DO WITH YOU HORRID CREATURES!
ERM, EVIL MASTER... DON'T YOU THINK WHAT YOU'RE DOING IS A LITTLE MEAN?
EUGENE...
I'M GOING TO PRETEND I DIDN'T HEAR WHAT YOU JUST SAID. NOW GET OUT BEFORE I TURN YOU INTO MARSHMALLOW ICE CREAM!
YES, EVIL MASTER.
THAT NIGHT...
PSSSST!
I KNEW I COULD COUNT ON YOU, MR. BUZZINGTON. HERE'S A TINY SCARF. IT'S COLD WHERE YOU'RE GOING...
BZZZZ
BZZZZZ
BZZZ
BZZZ
HEAVY...
BE SAFE, MR. BUZZINGTON!
BZZZ
ANTARCTICA: EEP'S HQ
GAAAAAH! GET IT OUT! IT'S GOING TO STING ME! I SEE DEATH IN ITS EYES!
SIR, IT'S JUST A TINY BEE... WAIT... LOOK, IT'S HOLDING SOMETHING.
IT'S AN ENVELOPE.
BRRZZZZ
BRRZZZZ
Dear Number 8, Don't show this to EEP He won't trust it... Ruth is locked away, I can help you save her. Use coordinates 3, 19, 81, 2 to find Evil Cat's base. from ? x
P.S. I miss you.

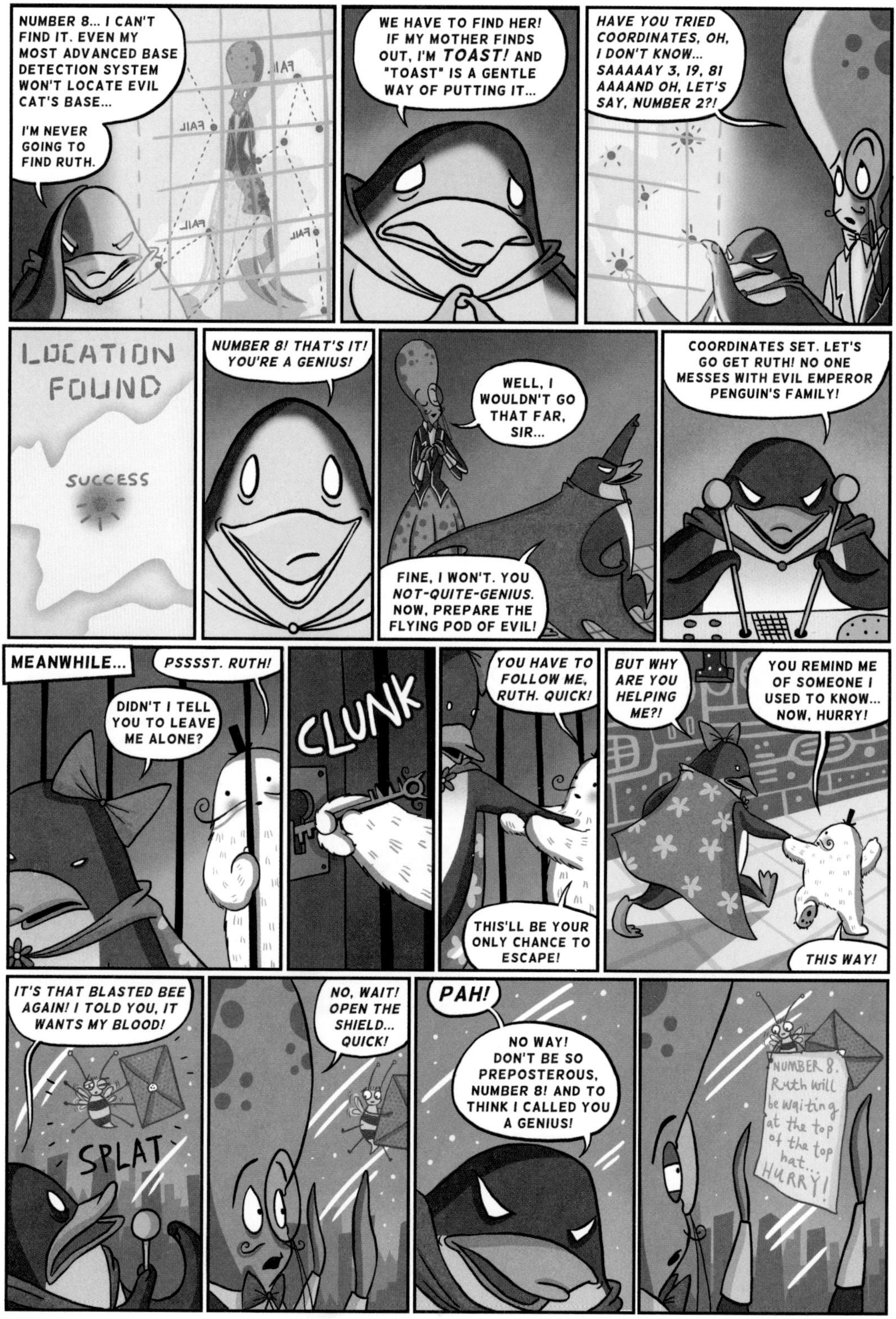
NUMBER 8... I CAN'T FIND IT. EVEN MY MOST ADVANCED BASE DETECTION SYSTEM WON'T LOCATE EVIL CAT'S BASE...
I'M NEVER GOING TO FIND RUTH.
WE HAVE TO FIND HER! IF MY MOTHER FINDS OUT, I'M *TOAST!* AND "TOAST" IS A GENTLE WAY OF PUTTING IT...
HAVE YOU TRIED COORDINATES, OH, I DON'T KNOW... SAAAAAY 3, 19, 81 AAAAND OH, LET'S SAY, NUMBER 2?!
LOCATION FOUND
SUCCESS
NUMBER 8! THAT'S IT! YOU'RE A GENIUS!
WELL, I WOULDN'T GO THAT FAR, SIR...
FINE, I WON'T. YOU *NOT-QUITE-GENIUS.* NOW, PREPARE THE FLYING POD OF EVIL!
COORDINATES SET. LET'S GO GET RUTH! NO ONE MESSES WITH EVIL EMPEROR PENGUIN'S FAMILY!
MEANWHILE...
PSSSST. RUTH!
DIDN'T I TELL YOU TO LEAVE ME ALONE?
CLUNK
YOU HAVE TO FOLLOW ME, RUTH. QUICK!
THIS'LL BE YOUR ONLY CHANCE TO ESCAPE!
BUT WHY ARE YOU HELPING ME?!
YOU REMIND ME OF SOMEONE I USED TO KNOW... NOW, HURRY!
THIS WAY!
IT'S THAT BLASTED BEE AGAIN! I TOLD YOU, IT WANTS MY BLOOD!
SPLAT
NO, WAIT! OPEN THE SHIELD... QUICK!
PAH!
NO WAY! DON'T BE SO PREPOSTEROUS, NUMBER 8! AND TO THINK I CALLED YOU A GENIUS!
NUMBER 8. Ruth will be waiting at the top of the top hat... HURRY!

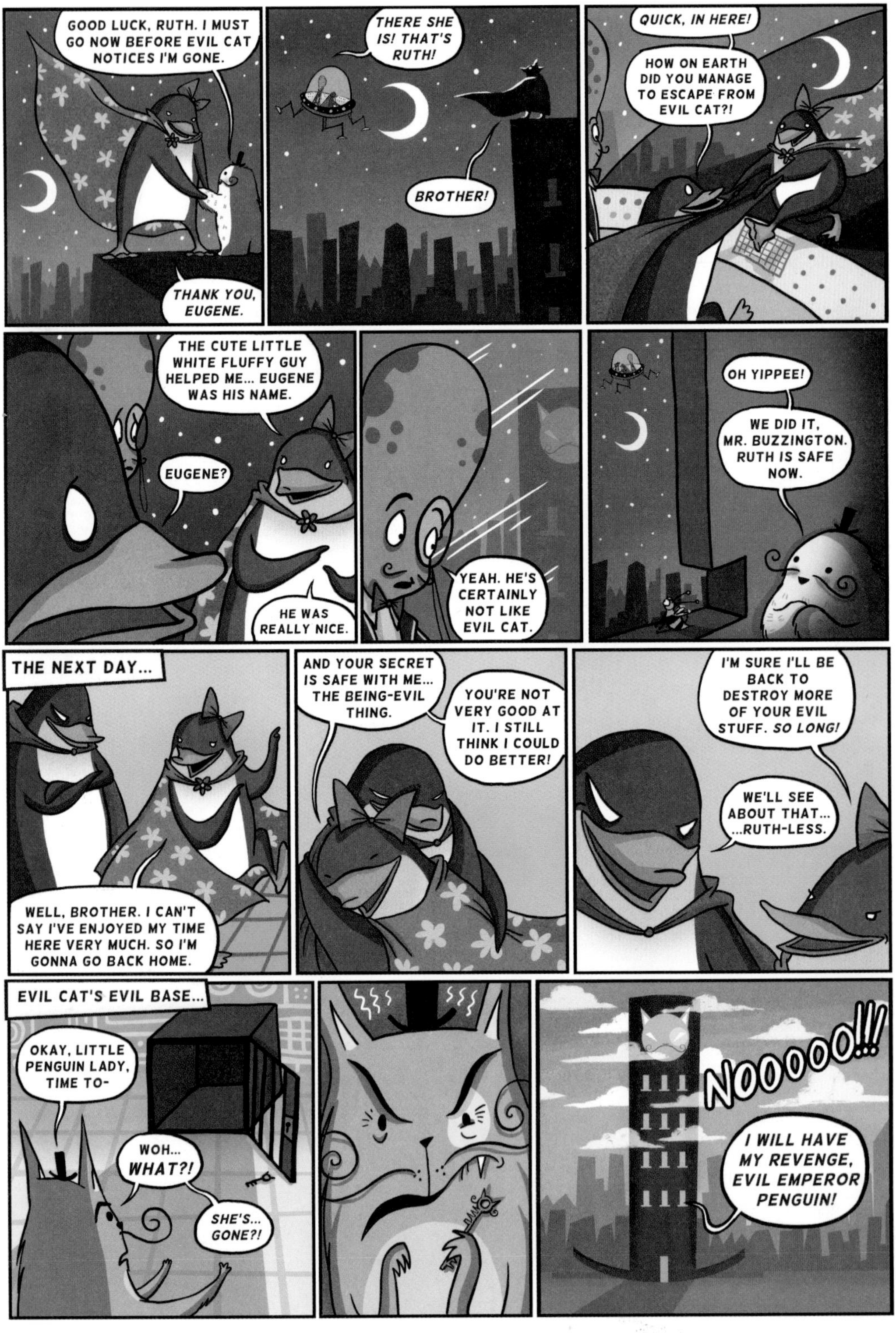

GOOD LUCK, RUTH. I MUST GO NOW BEFORE EVIL CAT NOTICES I'M GONE.
THANK YOU, EUGENE.
THERE SHE IS! THAT'S RUTH!
BROTHER!
QUICK, IN HERE!
HOW ON EARTH DID YOU MANAGE TO ESCAPE FROM EVIL CAT?!
THE CUTE LITTLE WHITE FLUFFY GUY HELPED ME... EUGENE WAS HIS NAME.
EUGENE?
HE WAS REALLY NICE.
YEAH. HE'S CERTAINLY NOT LIKE EVIL CAT.
OH YIPPEE!
WE DID IT, MR. BUZZINGTON. RUTH IS SAFE NOW.
THE NEXT DAY...
WELL, BROTHER. I CAN'T SAY I'VE ENJOYED MY TIME HERE VERY MUCH. SO I'M GONNA GO BACK HOME.
AND YOUR SECRET IS SAFE WITH ME... THE BEING-EVIL THING.
YOU'RE NOT VERY GOOD AT IT. I STILL THINK I COULD DO BETTER!
I'M SURE I'LL BE BACK TO DESTROY MORE OF YOUR EVIL STUFF. SO LONG!
WE'LL SEE ABOUT THAT... ...RUTH-LESS.
EVIL CAT'S EVIL BASE...
OKAY, LITTLE PENGUIN LADY, TIME TO-
WOH... WHAT?!
SHE'S... GONE?!
NOOOOO!!!
I WILL HAVE MY REVENGE, EVIL EMPEROR PENGUIN!

The Return: Part 1

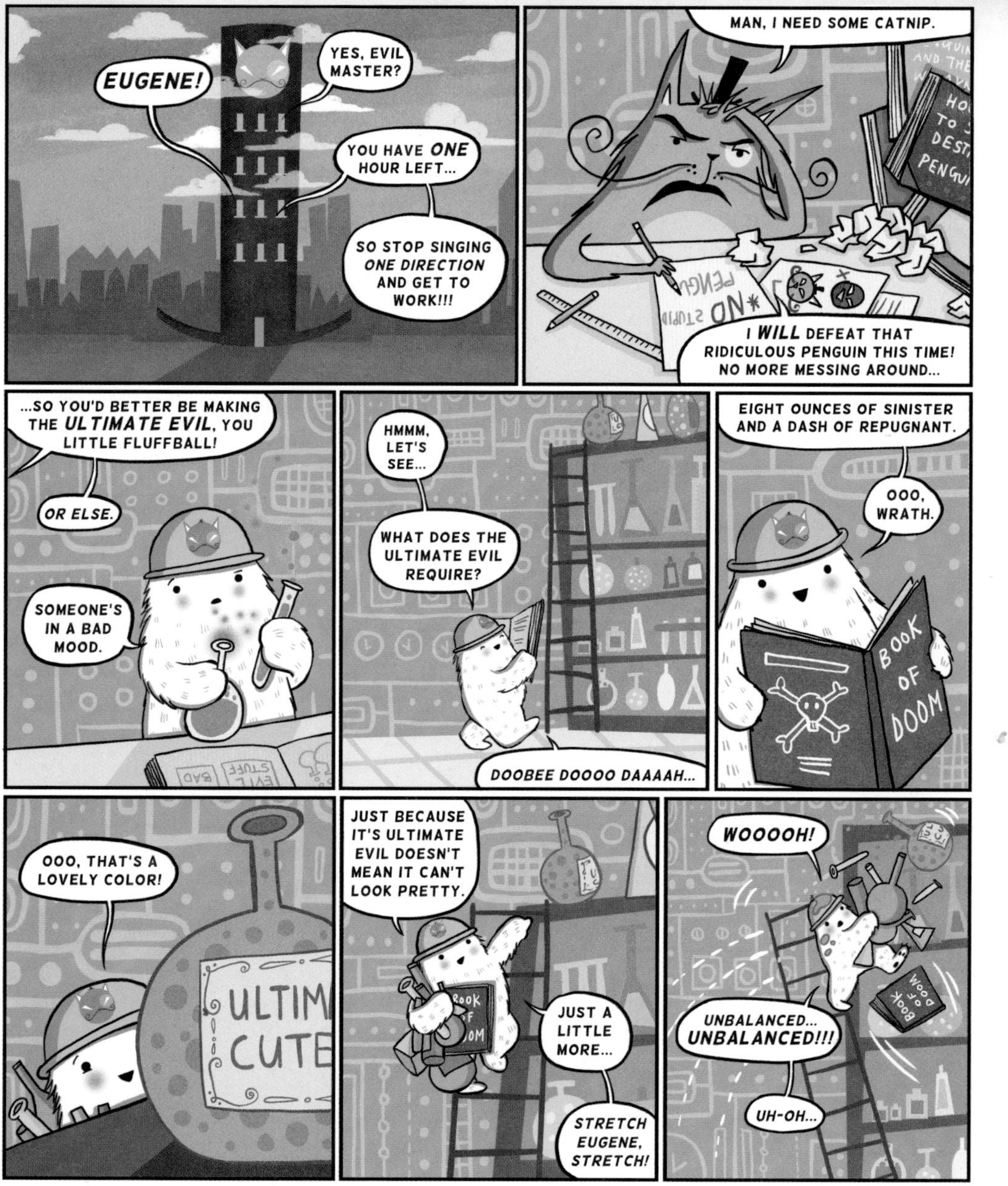
EUGENE!
YES, EVIL MASTER?
YOU HAVE ONE HOUR LEFT...
SO STOP SINGING ONE DIRECTION AND GET TO WORK!!!
MAN, I NEED SOME CATNIP.
I WILL DEFEAT THAT RIDICULOUS PENGUIN THIS TIME! NO MORE MESSING AROUND...
...SO YOU'D BETTER BE MAKING THE ULTIMATE EVIL, YOU LITTLE FLUFFBALL!
OR ELSE.
SOMEONE'S IN A BAD MOOD.
HMMM, LET'S SEE...
WHAT DOES THE ULTIMATE EVIL REQUIRE?
DOOBEE DOOOO DAAAAH...
EIGHT OUNCES OF SINISTER AND A DASH OF REPUGNANT.
OOO, WRATH.
BOOK OF DOOM
OOO, THAT'S A LOVELY COLOR!
ULTIM
CUTE
JUST BECAUSE IT'S ULTIMATE EVIL DOESN'T MEAN IT CAN'T LOOK PRETTY.
JUST A LITTLE MORE...
STRETCH EUGENE, STRETCH!
WOOOOH!
UNBALANCED... UNBALANCED!!!
UH-OH...

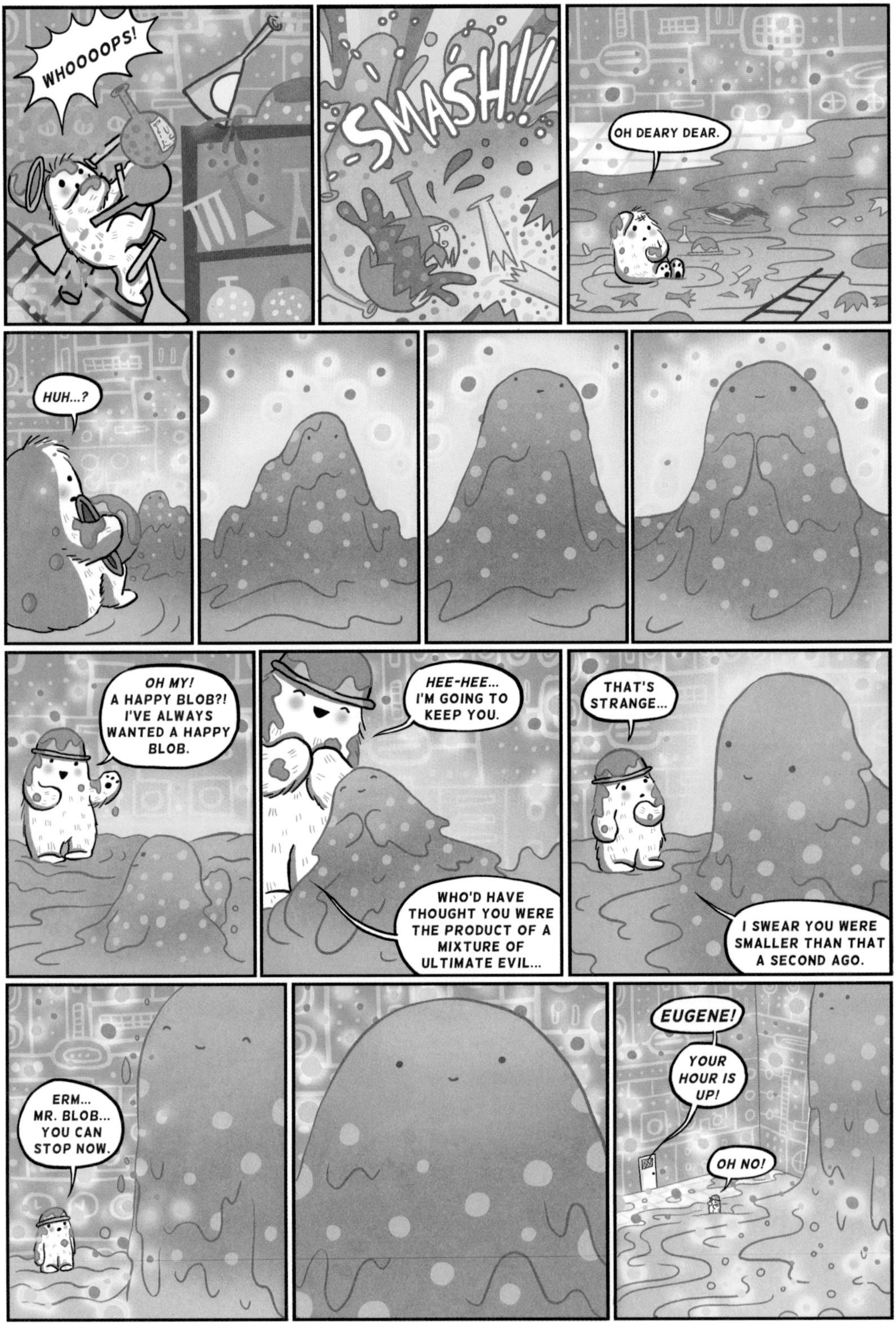
WHOOOOPS!
SMASH!!
OH DEARY DEAR.
HUH...?
OH MY! A HAPPY BLOB?! I'VE ALWAYS WANTED A HAPPY BLOB.
HEE-HEE... I'M GOING TO KEEP YOU.
WHO'D HAVE THOUGHT YOU WERE THE PRODUCT OF A MIXTURE OF ULTIMATE EVIL...
THAT'S STRANGE...
I SWEAR YOU WERE SMALLER THAN THAT A SECOND AGO.
ERM... MR. BLOB... YOU CAN STOP NOW.
EUGENE!
YOUR HOUR IS UP!
OH NO!

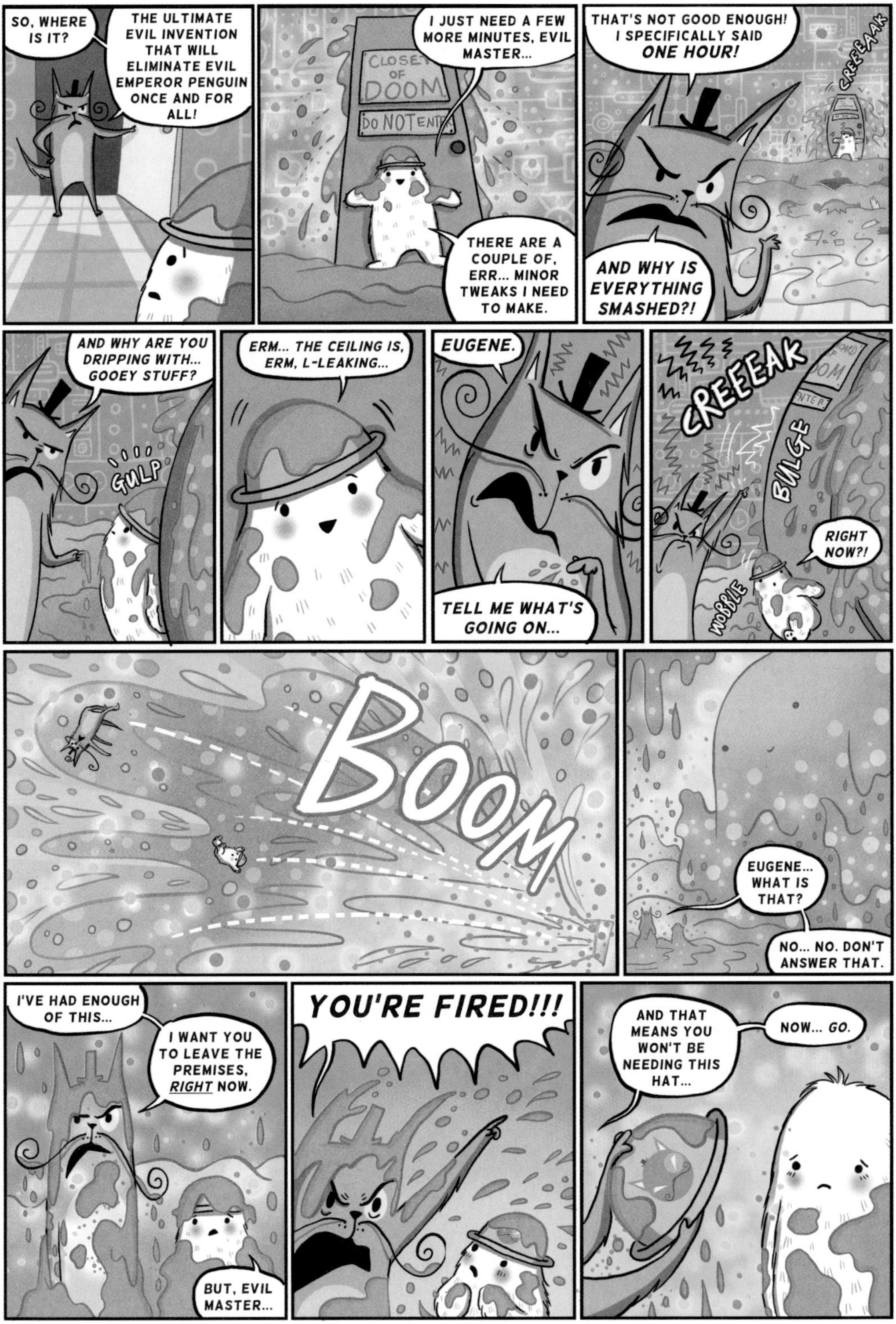
SO, WHERE IS IT?
THE ULTIMATE EVIL INVENTION THAT WILL ELIMINATE EVIL EMPEROR PENGUIN ONCE AND FOR ALL!
I JUST NEED A FEW MORE MINUTES, EVIL MASTER...
CLOSET OF DOOM
DO NOT ENTER
THERE ARE A COUPLE OF, ERR... MINOR TWEAKS I NEED TO MAKE.
THAT'S NOT GOOD ENOUGH! I SPECIFICALLY SAID ONE HOUR!
CREEEAAK
AND WHY IS EVERYTHING SMASHED?!
AND WHY ARE YOU DRIPPING WITH... GOOEY STUFF?
GULP
ERM... THE CEILING IS, ERM, L-LEAKING...
EUGENE.
TELL ME WHAT'S GOING ON...
CREEEAK
BULGE
RIGHT NOW?!
WOBBLE
BOOM
EUGENE... WHAT IS THAT?
NO... NO. DON'T ANSWER THAT.
I'VE HAD ENOUGH OF THIS...
I WANT YOU TO LEAVE THE PREMISES, RIGHT NOW.
BUT, EVIL MASTER...
YOU'RE FIRED!!!
AND THAT MEANS YOU WON'T BE NEEDING THIS HAT...
NOW... GO.

THE RETURN: PART 2

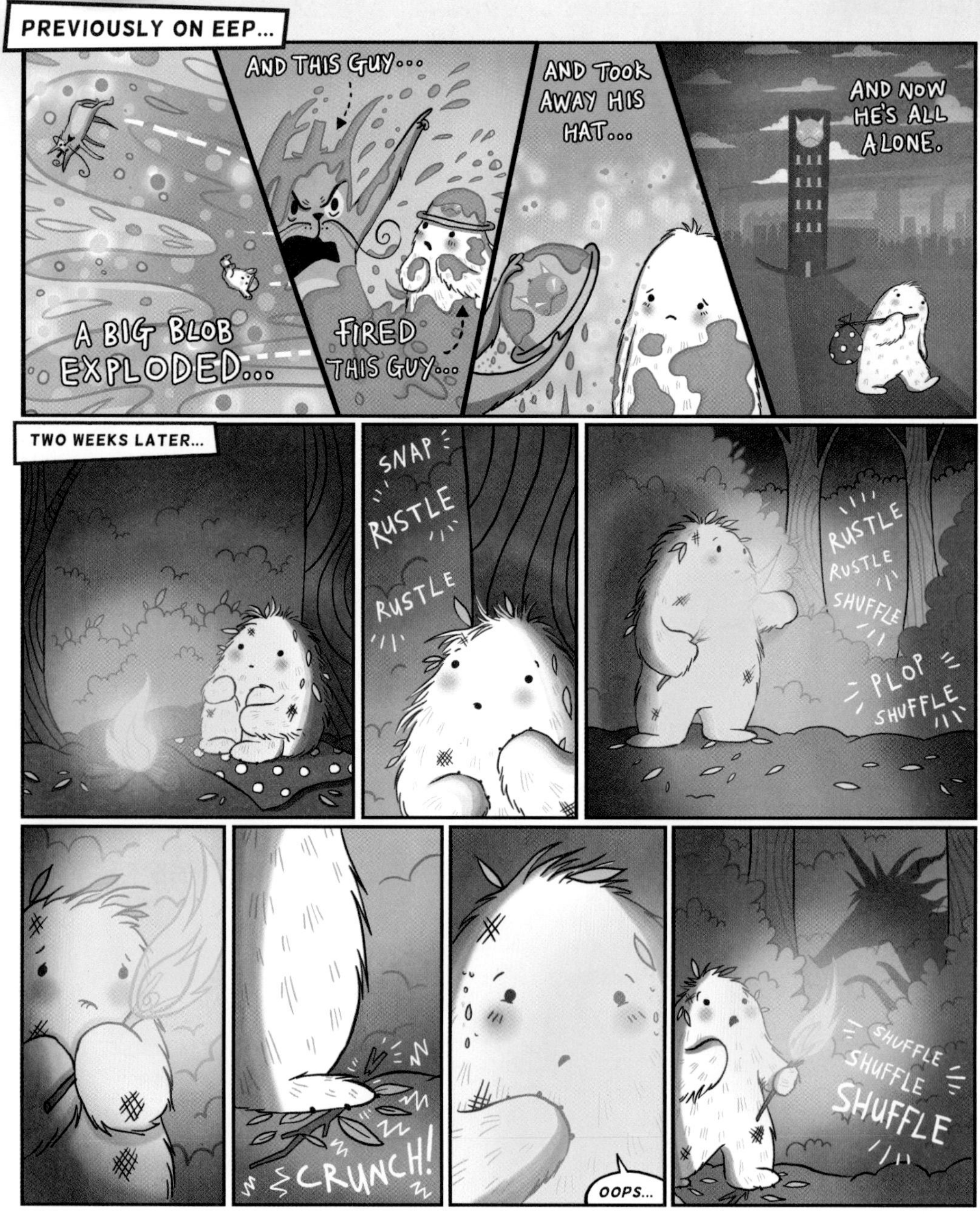

PREVIOUSLY ON EEP...
A BIG BLOB EXPLODED...
AND THIS GUY...
FIRED THIS GUY...
AND TOOK AWAY HIS HAT...
AND NOW HE'S ALL ALONE.
TWO WEEKS LATER...
SNAP
RUSTLE
RUSTLE
RUSTLE
RUSTLE
SHUFFLE
PLOP
SHUFFLE
CRUNCH!
OOPS...
SHUFFLE
SHUFFLE
SHUFFLE

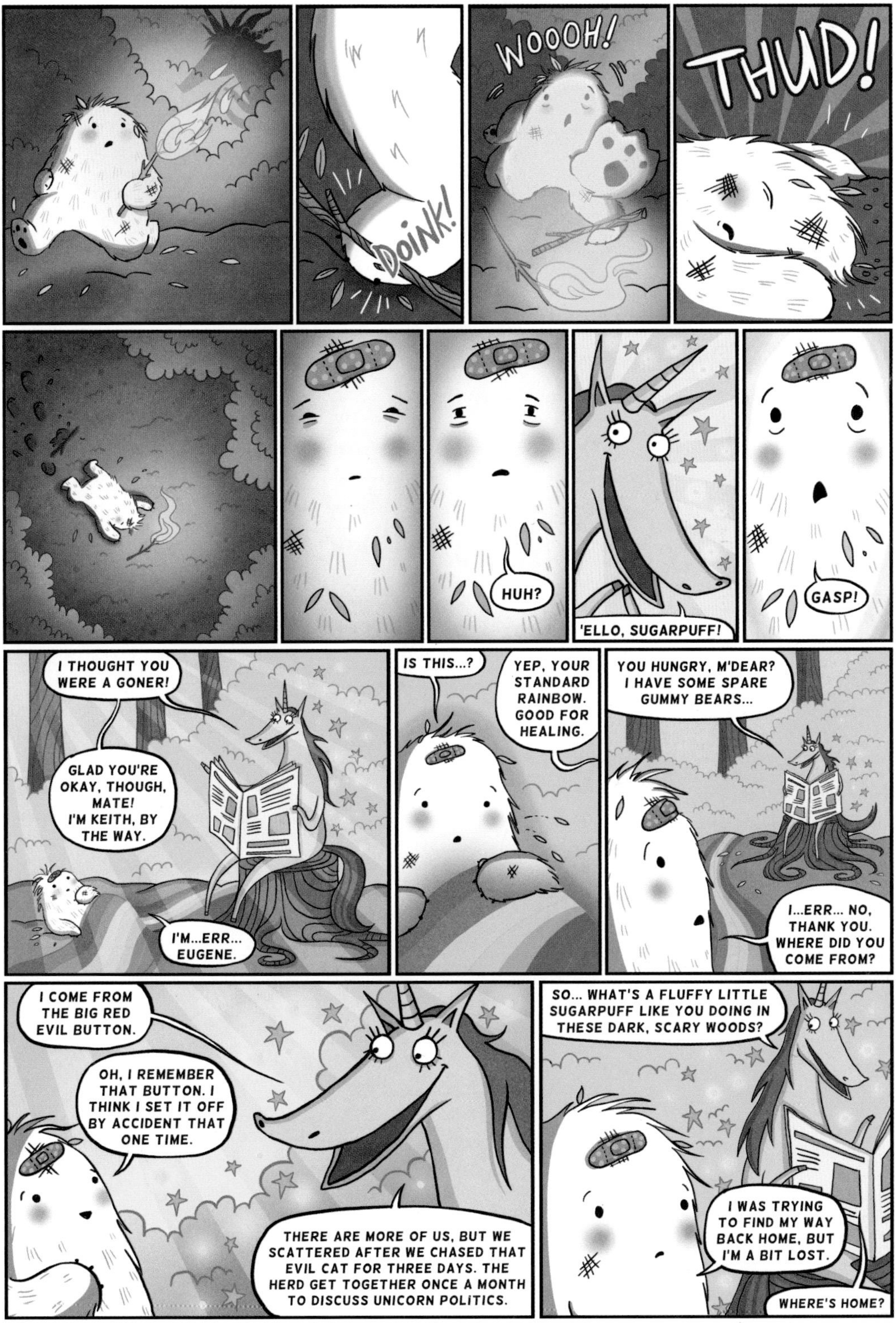

WOOOH!
DOINK!
THUD!
HUH?
'ELLO, SUGARPUFF!
GASP!
I THOUGHT YOU WERE A GONER!
GLAD YOU'RE OKAY, THOUGH, MATE! I'M KEITH, BY THE WAY.
I'M...ERR... EUGENE.
IS THIS...?
YEP, YOUR STANDARD RAINBOW. GOOD FOR HEALING.
YOU HUNGRY, M'DEAR? I HAVE SOME SPARE GUMMY BEARS...
I...ERR... NO, THANK YOU. WHERE DID YOU COME FROM?
I COME FROM THE BIG RED EVIL BUTTON.
OH, I REMEMBER THAT BUTTON. I THINK I SET IT OFF BY ACCIDENT THAT ONE TIME.
THERE ARE MORE OF US, BUT WE SCATTERED AFTER WE CHASED THAT EVIL CAT FOR THREE DAYS. THE HERD GET TOGETHER ONCE A MONTH TO DISCUSS UNICORN POLITICS.
SO... WHAT'S A FLUFFY LITTLE SUGARPUFF LIKE YOU DOING IN THESE DARK, SCARY WOODS?
I WAS TRYING TO FIND MY WAY BACK HOME, BUT I'M A BIT LOST.
WHERE'S HOME?

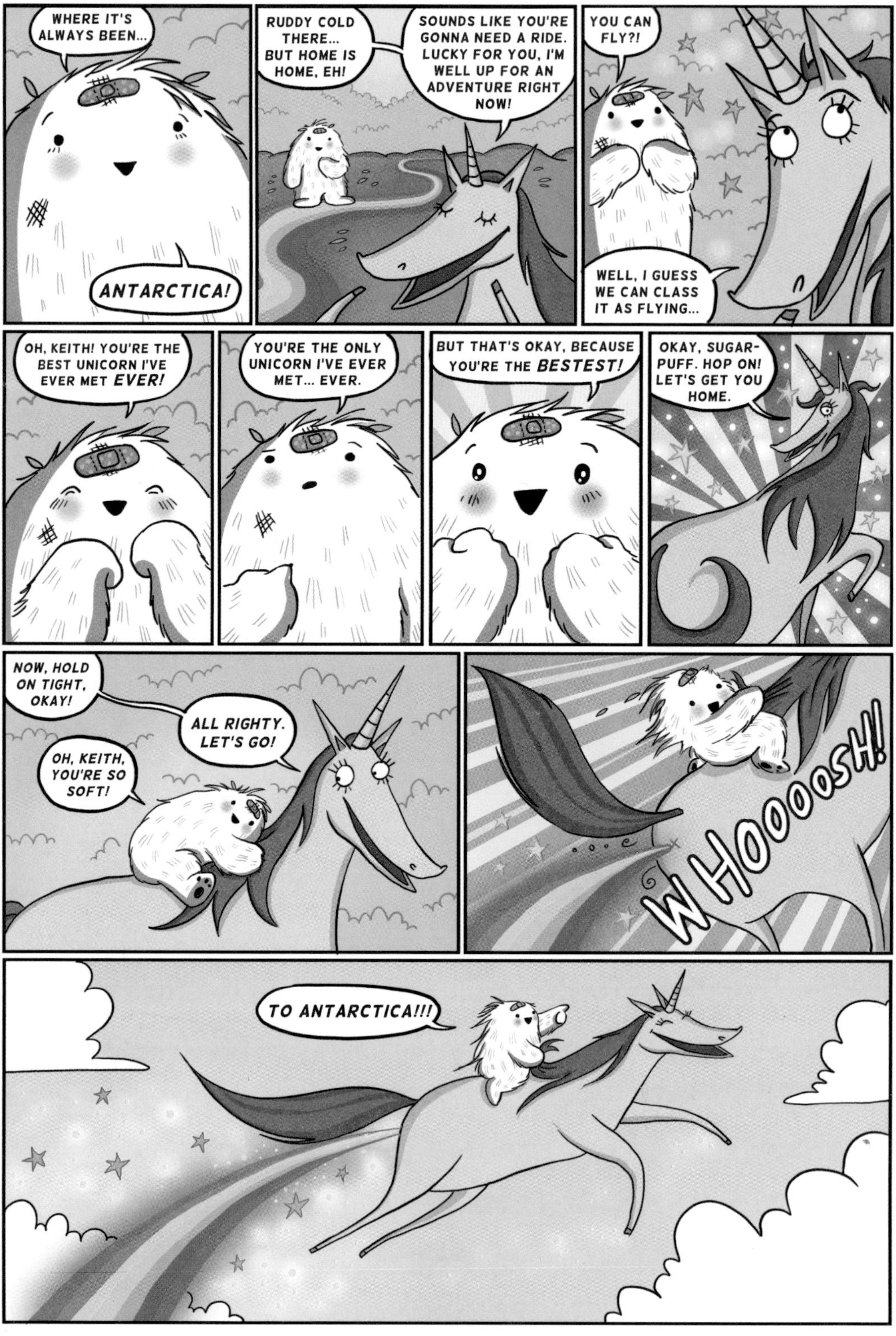
WHERE IT'S ALWAYS BEEN...
ANTARCTICA!
RUDDY COLD THERE... BUT HOME IS HOME, EH!
SOUNDS LIKE YOU'RE GONNA NEED A RIDE. LUCKY FOR YOU, I'M WELL UP FOR AN ADVENTURE RIGHT NOW!
YOU CAN FLY?!
WELL, I GUESS WE CAN CLASS IT AS FLYING...
OH, KEITH! YOU'RE THE BEST UNICORN I'VE EVER MET EVER!
YOU'RE THE ONLY UNICORN I'VE EVER MET... EVER.
BUT THAT'S OKAY, BECAUSE YOU'RE THE BESTEST!
OKAY, SUGAR-PUFF. HOP ON! LET'S GET YOU HOME.
NOW, HOLD ON TIGHT, OKAY!
ALL RIGHTY. LET'S GO!
OH, KEITH, YOU'RE SO SOFT!
WHOOOOSH!
TO ANTARCTICA!!!

THE RETURN: PART 3

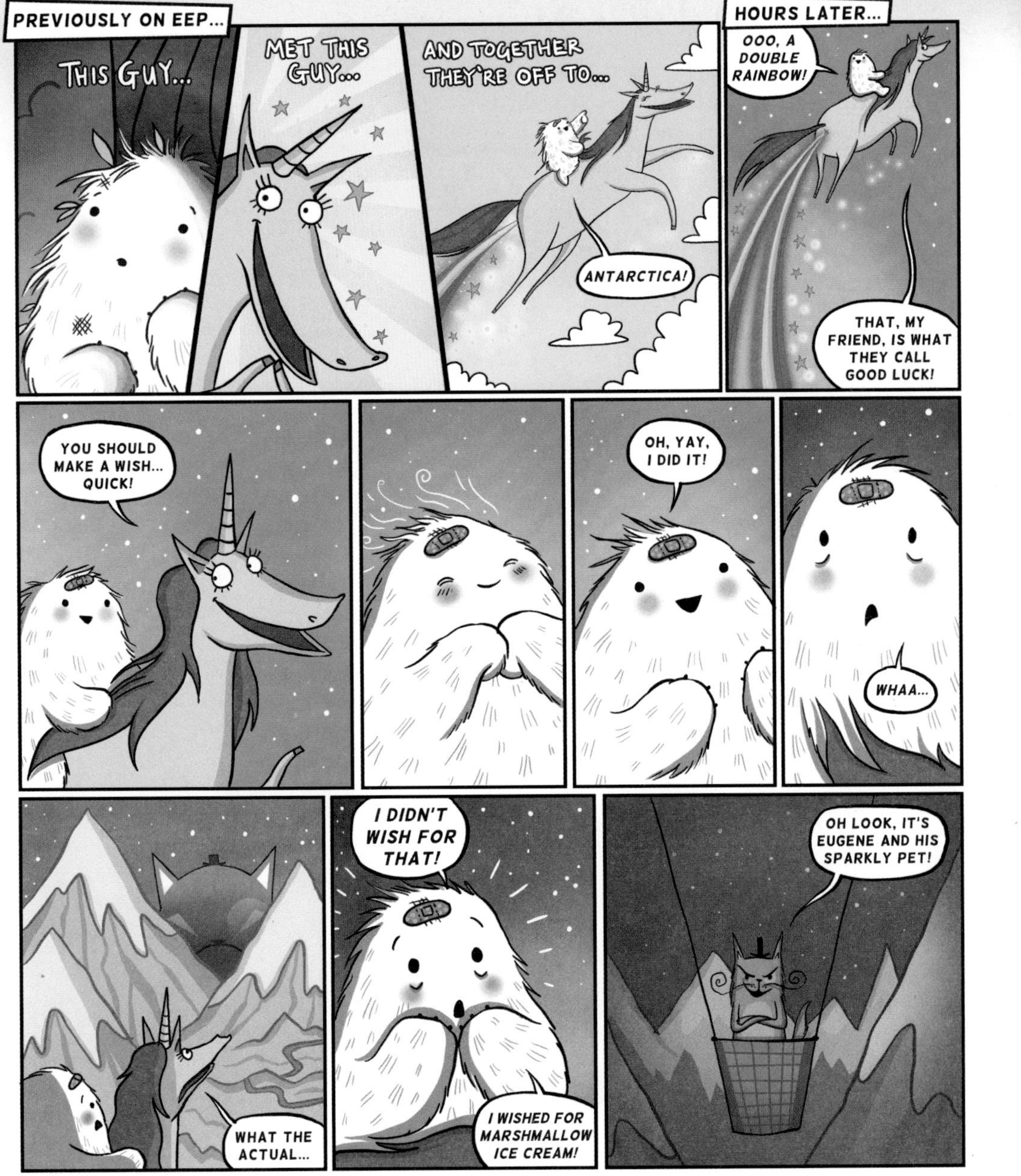
PREVIOUSLY ON EEP...
THIS GUY...
MET THIS GUY...
AND TOGETHER THEY'RE OFF TO...
ANTARCTICA!
HOURS LATER...
OOO, A DOUBLE RAINBOW!
THAT, MY FRIEND, IS WHAT THEY CALL GOOD LUCK!
YOU SHOULD MAKE A WISH... QUICK!
OH, YAY, I DID IT!
WHAA...
WHAT THE ACTUAL...
I DIDN'T WISH FOR THAT!
I WISHED FOR MARSHMALLOW ICE CREAM!
OH LOOK, IT'S EUGENE AND HIS SPARKLY PET!

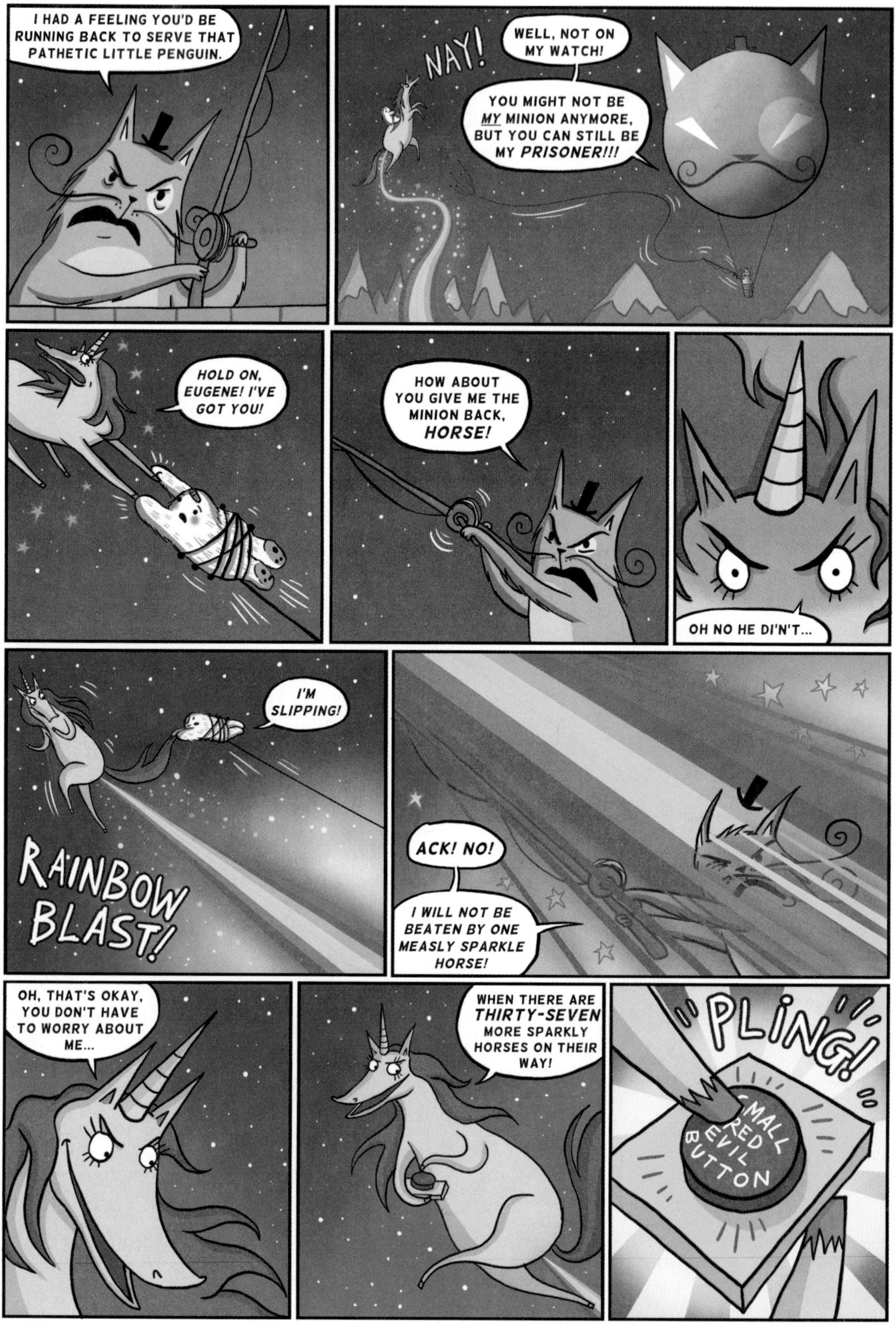
I HAD A FEELING YOU'D BE RUNNING BACK TO SERVE THAT PATHETIC LITTLE PENGUIN.
NAY!
WELL, NOT ON MY WATCH!
YOU MIGHT NOT BE MY MINION ANYMORE, BUT YOU CAN STILL BE MY PRISONER!!!
HOLD ON, EUGENE! I'VE GOT YOU!
HOW ABOUT YOU GIVE ME THE MINION BACK, HORSE!
OH NO HE DI'N'T...
I'M SLIPPING!
RAINBOW BLAST!
ACK! NO!
I WILL NOT BE BEATEN BY ONE MEASLY SPARKLE HORSE!
OH, THAT'S OKAY, YOU DON'T HAVE TO WORRY ABOUT ME...
WHEN THERE ARE THIRTY-SEVEN MORE SPARKLY HORSES ON THEIR WAY!
PLING!
SMALL RED EVIL BUTTON

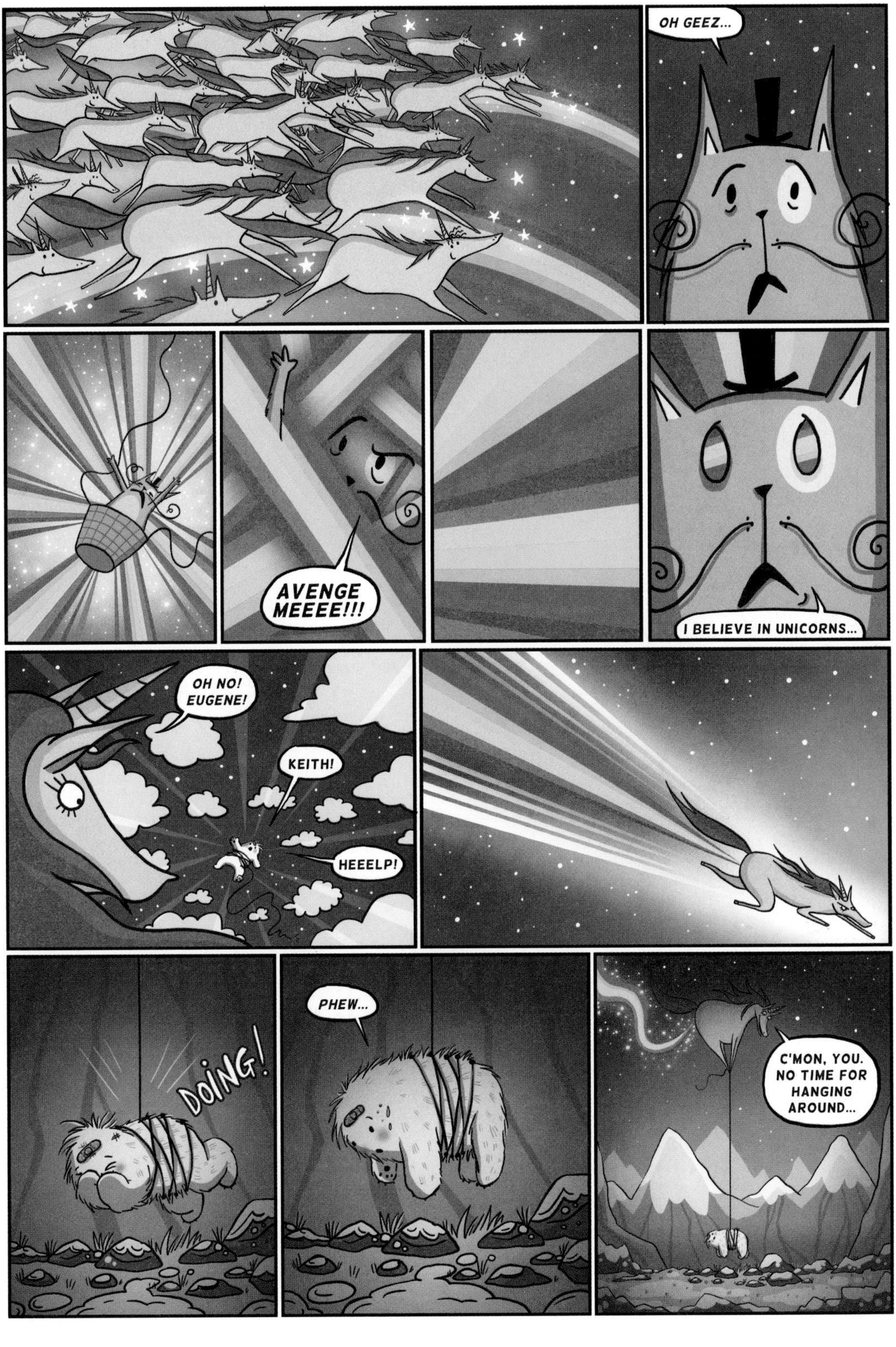
OH GEEZ...
AVENGE MEEEE!!!
I BELIEVE IN UNICORNS...
OH NO! EUGENE!
KEITH!
HEEELP!
DOING!
PHEW...
C'MON, YOU. NO TIME FOR HANGING AROUND...

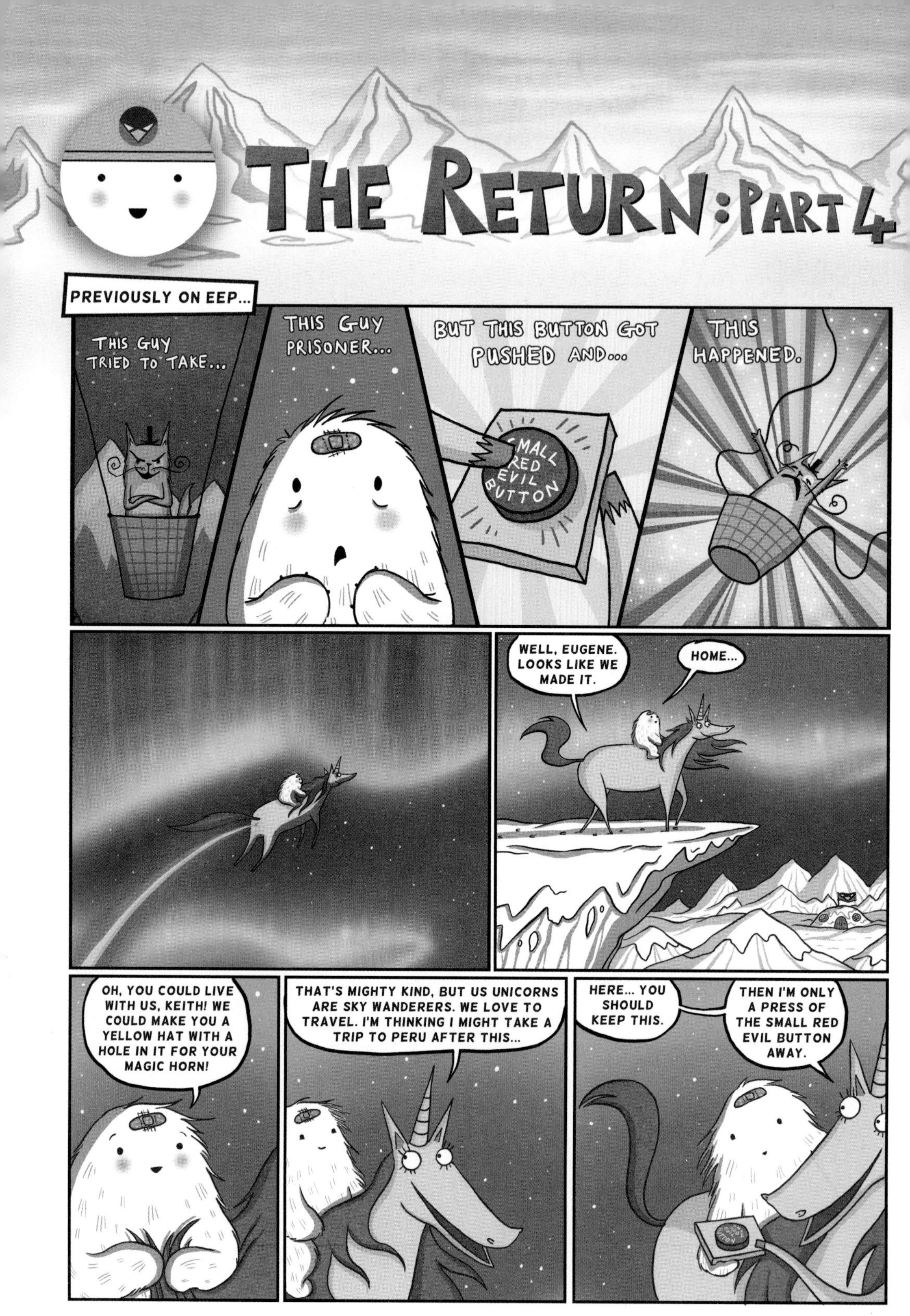
THE RETURN: PART 4
PREVIOUSLY ON EEP...
THIS GUY TRIED TO TAKE...
THIS GUY PRISONER...
BUT THIS BUTTON GOT PUSHED AND...
SMALL RED EVIL BUTTON
THIS HAPPENED.
WELL, EUGENE. LOOKS LIKE WE MADE IT.
HOME...
OH, YOU COULD LIVE WITH US, KEITH! WE COULD MAKE YOU A YELLOW HAT WITH A HOLE IN IT FOR YOUR MAGIC HORN!
THAT'S MIGHTY KIND, BUT US UNICORNS ARE SKY WANDERERS. WE LOVE TO TRAVEL. I'M THINKING I MIGHT TAKE A TRIP TO PERU AFTER THIS...
HERE... YOU SHOULD KEEP THIS.
THEN I'M ONLY A PRESS OF THE SMALL RED EVIL BUTTON AWAY.

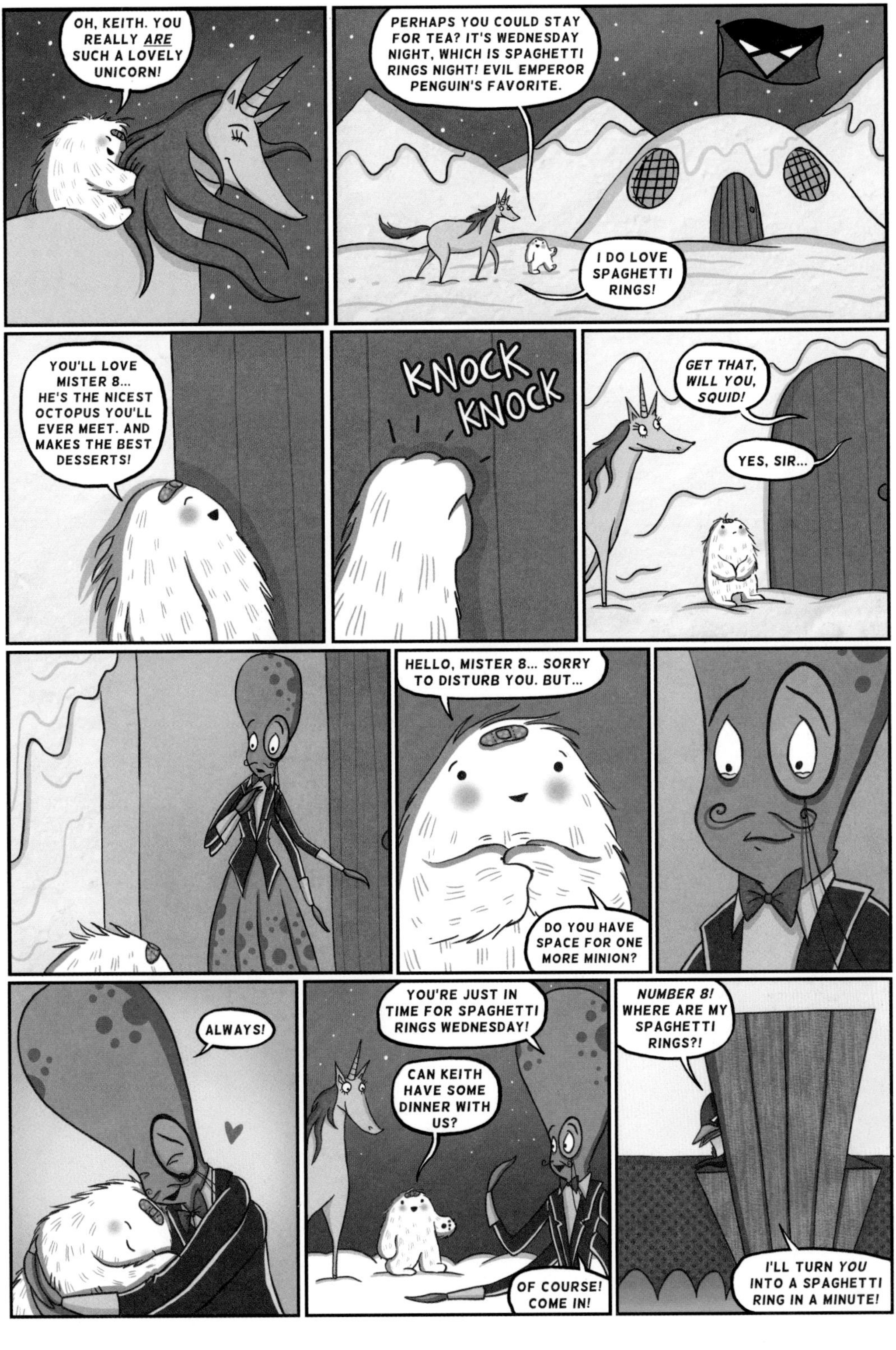
OH, KEITH. YOU REALLY *ARE* SUCH A LOVELY UNICORN!
PERHAPS YOU COULD STAY FOR TEA? IT'S WEDNESDAY NIGHT, WHICH IS SPAGHETTI RINGS NIGHT! EVIL EMPEROR PENGUIN'S FAVORITE.
I DO LOVE SPAGHETTI RINGS!
YOU'LL LOVE MISTER 8... HE'S THE NICEST OCTOPUS YOU'LL EVER MEET. AND MAKES THE BEST DESSERTS!
KNOCK KNOCK
GET THAT, WILL YOU, SQUID!
YES, SIR...
HELLO, MISTER 8... SORRY TO DISTURB YOU. BUT...
DO YOU HAVE SPACE FOR ONE MORE MINION?
ALWAYS!
YOU'RE JUST IN TIME FOR SPAGHETTI RINGS WEDNESDAY!
CAN KEITH HAVE SOME DINNER WITH US?
OF COURSE! COME IN!
NUMBER 8! WHERE ARE MY SPAGHETTI RINGS?!
I'LL TURN *YOU* INTO A SPAGHETTI RING IN A MINUTE!

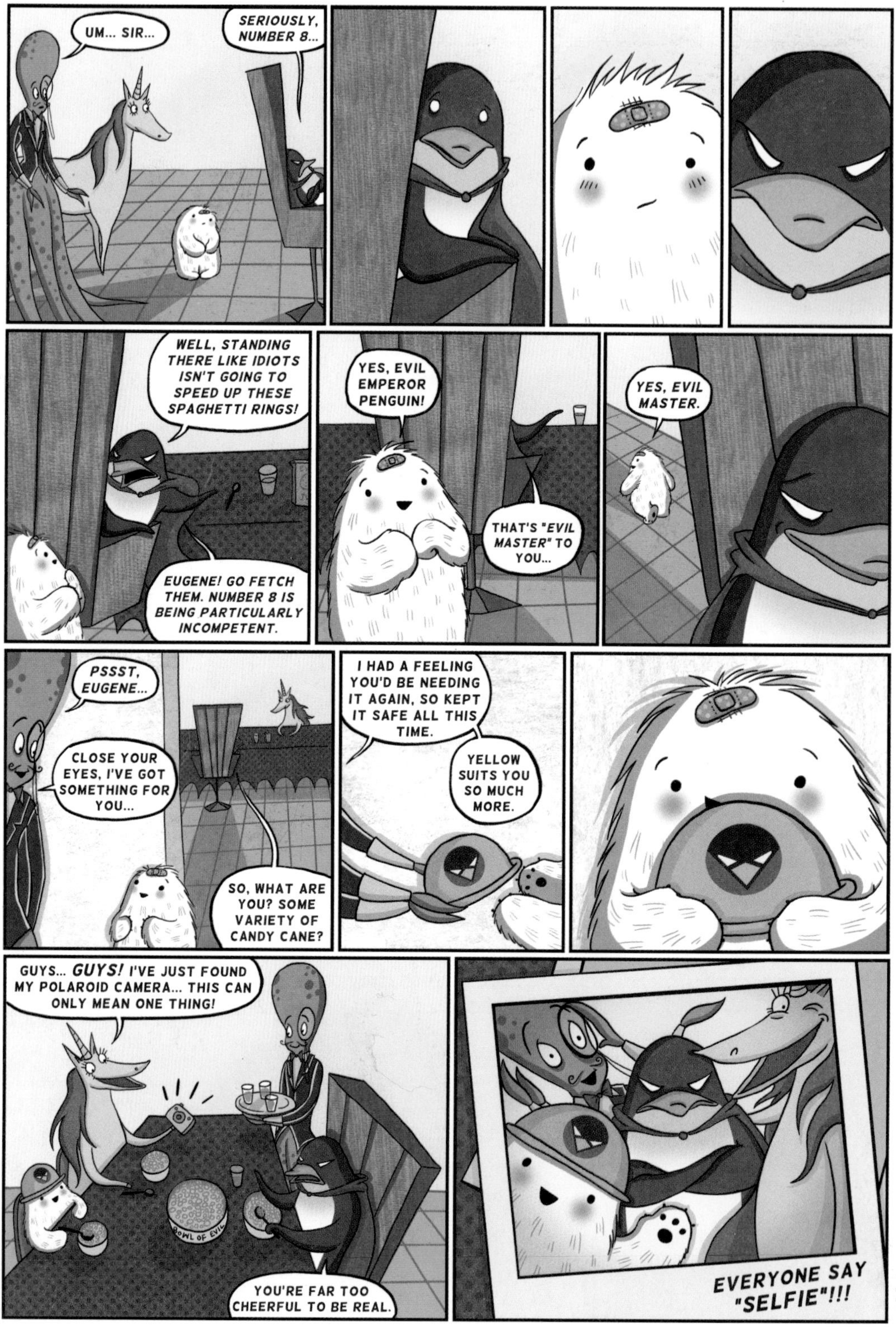
UM... SIR...
SERIOUSLY, NUMBER 8...
WELL, STANDING THERE LIKE IDIOTS ISN'T GOING TO SPEED UP THESE SPAGHETTI RINGS!
EUGENE! GO FETCH THEM. NUMBER 8 IS BEING PARTICULARLY INCOMPETENT.
YES, EVIL EMPEROR PENGUIN!
THAT'S "EVIL MASTER" TO YOU...
YES, EVIL MASTER.
PSSST, EUGENE...
CLOSE YOUR EYES, I'VE GOT SOMETHING FOR YOU...
SO, WHAT ARE YOU? SOME VARIETY OF CANDY CANE?
I HAD A FEELING YOU'D BE NEEDING IT AGAIN, SO KEPT IT SAFE ALL THIS TIME.
YELLOW SUITS YOU SO MUCH MORE.
GUYS... GUYS! I'VE JUST FOUND MY POLAROID CAMERA... THIS CAN ONLY MEAN ONE THING!
BOWL OF EVIL
YOU'RE FAR TOO CHEERFUL TO BE REAL.
EVERYONE SAY "SELFIE"!!!